MONKEYS

SUSAN MINOT

MONKEYS

E. P. DUTTON / SEYMOUR LAWRENCE
NEW YORK

The following stories originally appeared in The New Yorker:
"Allowance," "Accident," and "Thorofare."
"Hiding," "Thanksgiving Day," "The Navigator," and "Wedlock"
(which appeared under the title "The Silver Box") first appeared in
Grand Street.

Published in the United States by E. P. Dutton / Seymour Lawrence,
a division of New American Library,
2 Park Avenue, New York, N.Y. 10016.

Library of Congress Cataloging-in-Publication Data
Minot, Susan.
Monkeys.
I. Title.
PS3563.I4755M6   1986   813'.54   85–30775

ISBN: 0-525-24342-9

Published simultaneously in Canada
by Fitzhenry and Whiteside, Limited, Toronto.
COBE
Designed by Steven N. Stathakis

10 9 8 7 6 5 4 3 2 1

First Edition

To my family
to the memory of my mother
and
to Ben Sonnenberg

ACKNOWLEDGMENTS

The author wishes to thank the following whose guidance and generosity helped sustain her in the writing of this book: her publisher Seymour Lawrence; Jean and Gordon Douglas; Mrs. Douglas Auchincloss; Dr. Daniel Schneider; Nancy Lemann; her editors at *The New Yorker,* Trish Deitch and Daniel Menaker; Gary Fisketjon; the people at *Grand Street;* the MacDowell Colony; Yaddo; and JMS.

The houses are all gone under the sea.

—T. S. ELIOT

CONTENTS

THE FAMILY

Augustus Paine Vincent (Gus)

Rosie Vincent, née Rose Marie O'Dare

THEIR CHILDREN

Caitlin Marie Vincent

Sophie O'Dare Vincent

Delilah Lothrop Vincent

Augustus Paine Vincent, Jr.   (Gus)

Donald Sherman Vincent   (Sherman)

Chase Endicott Vincent   (Chicky)

Miranda Rose Vincent   (Minnie)

HIDING

Our father doesn't go to church with us but we're all downstairs in the hall at the same time, bumbling, getting ready to go. Mum knuckles the buttons of Chicky's snowsuit till he's knot-tight, crouching, her heels lifted out of the backs of her shoes, her nylons creased at the ankles. She wears a black lace veil that stays on her hair like magic. Sherman ripples by, coat flapping, and Mum grabs him by the hood, reeling him in, and zips him up with a pinch at his chin. Gus stands there with his bottom lip out, waiting, looking like someone's smacked him except not that hard. Even though he's seven, he still wants Mum to do him up. Delilah comes half-hurrying down the stairs, late, looking like a ragamuffin with her skirt slid down to her hips and her hair all slept on wrong. Caitlin says, "It's about time." Delilah sweeps along the curve of the banister, looks at Caitlin, who's all ready to go herself with her pea jacket on and her loafers and bare legs, and tells her, "You're going to freeze." Everyone's in a bad mood because we just woke up.

Dad's outside already on the other side of the French doors, waiting for us to go. You can tell it's cold out there by his white breath blowing by his cheek in spurts. He just stands on the porch, hands shoved in his black parka, feet pressed together, looking at the crusty snow on the lawn. He doesn't wear a hat but that's because he barely feels the cold. Mum's the one who's warm-blooded. At skiing, she'll take you in when your toes get numb. You sit there with hot chocolate and a carton of french fries and the other mothers and she rubs your foot to get the circulation back. Down on the driveway the car is warming up and the exhaust goes straight up, disappearing in thin white curls.

"Okay, monkeys," says Mum filing us out the door. Chicky starts down the steps one red boot at a time till Mum whisks him up under a wing. The driveway is wrinkled over with ice so we take little shuffle steps across it, blinking at how bright it is, still only half-awake. Only the station wagon can fit everybody. Gus and Sherman scamper in across the huge backseat. Caitlin's head is the only one that shows over the front. (Caitlin is the oldest and she's eleven. I'm next, then Delilah, then the boys.) Mum rubs her thumbs on the steering wheel so that her gloves are shiny and round at the knuckles. Dad is doing things like checking the gutters, waiting till we leave. When we finally barrel down the hill, he turns and goes back into the house, which is big and empty now and quiet.

We keep our coats on in church. Except for the O'Shaunesseys, we have the most children in one pew. Dad only comes on Christmas and Easter, because he's not Catholic. A lot of times you only see the mothers there. When Dad stays at home, he does things like cuts prickles in the woods or tears up thorns, or rakes leaves for burning, or just stands around on the other side of the house by the lilacs, surveying his garden, wondering what to do next. We usually sit up near the front and there's a lot of kneeling near the end. One time Gus got his finger stuck in the diamond-shaped holes of the heating vent and Mum had to yank it out. When the man comes around for the collection, we each put in a nickel or a dime and the handle goes by like a rake. If Mum drops in a five-dollar bill, she'll pluck out a couple of bills for her change.

The church is huge. Out loud in the dead quiet, a

3

baby blares out "Dah-Dee." We giggle and Mum goes "Ssshhh" but smiles too. A baby always yells at the quietest part. Only the girls are old enough to go to Communion; you're not allowed to chew it. The priest's neck is peeling and I try not to look. "He leaves me cold," Mum says when we leave, touching her forehead with a fingertip after dipping it into the holy water.

On the way home, we pick up the paper at Cage's and a bag of eight lollipops—one for each of us, plus Mum and Dad, even though Dad never eats his. I choose root beer. Sherman crinkles his wrapper, shifting his eyes around to see if anyone's looking. Gus says, "Sherman, you have to wait till after breakfast." Sherman gives a fierce look and shoves it in his mouth. Up in front, Mum, flicking on the blinker, says, "Take that out," with eyes in the back of her head.

Depending on what time of year it is, we do different things on the weekends. In the fall we might go to Castle Hill and stop by the orchard in Ipswich for cider and apples and red licorice. Castle Hill is closed after the summer so there's nobody else there and it's all covered with leaves. Mum goes up to the windows on the terrace and tries to peer in, cupping her hands around her eyes and seeing curtains. We do things like roll down the hills, making our arms stiff like mummies, or climb around on the marble statues, which are really cold, or balance along the edge of the fountains without falling. Mum says "Be careful" even though there's no water in them, just red leaves plastered against the sides. When Dad notices us he yells, "Get down."

One garden has a ghost, according to Mum. A lady used to sneak out and meet her lover in the garden behind the grape trellis. Or she'd hide in the garden somewhere and he'd look for her and find her. But one night she crept out and he didn't come and didn't come and finally when she couldn't stand it any longer, she went crazy and ran off the cliff and killed herself and now her ghost comes back and keeps waiting. We creep into the boxed-in place, smelling the yellow berries and the wet bark, and Delilah jumps—"What was that?"—trying to scare us. Dad shakes the wood to see if it's rotten. We run ahead and hide in a pile of leaves. Little twigs get in your mouth and your nostrils; we hold still underneath listening to the brittle ticking leaves. When we hear Mum and Dad get close, we burst up to surprise them, all the leaves fluttering down, sputtering from the dust and tiny grits that get all over your face like gray ash, like Ash Wednesday. Mum and Dad just keep walking. She brushes a pine needle from his collar and he jerks his head, thinking of something else, probably that it's a fly. We follow them back to the car in a line, all scruffy with leaf scraps.

After church, we have breakfast because you're not allowed to eat before. Dad comes in for the paper or a sliver of bacon. One thing about Dad, he has the weirdest taste. Spam is his favorite thing or this cheese that no one can stand the smell of. He barely sits down at all, glancing at the paper with his feet flat down on either side of him, ready to get up any minute to go back outside and sprinkle white fertilizer on the lawn. After, it looks like frost.

This Sunday we get to go skating at Ice House Pond. Dad drives. "Pipe down," he says into the backseat. Mum faces him with white fur around her hood. She calls him Uncs, short for Uncle, a kind of joke, I guess, calling him Uncs while he calls her Mum, same as we do. We are making a racket.

"Will you quit it?" Caitlin elbows Gus.

"What? I'm not doing anything."

"Just taking up all the room."

Sherman's in the way back. "How come Chicky always gets the front?"

" 'Cause he's the baby." Delilah is always explaining everything.

"I en not a baby," says Chicky without turning around.

Caitlin frowns at me. "Who said you could wear my scarf?"

6

I ask into the front seat, "Can we go to the Fairy Garden?" even though I know we won't.

"Why couldn't Rummy come?"

Delilah says, "Because Dad didn't want him to."

Sherman wants to know how old Dad was when he learned how to skate.

Dad says, "About your age." He has a deep voice.

"Really?" I think about that for a minute, about Dad being Sherman's age.

"What about Mum?" says Caitlin.

This isn't his department so he just keeps driving. Mum shifts her shoulders more toward us but still looks at Dad.

"When I was a little girl on the Boston Common." Her teeth are white and she wears fuchsia lipstick. "We used to have skating parties."

Caitlin leans close to Mum's fur hood, crossing her arms into a pillow. "What? With dates?"

Mum bats her eyelashes. "Oh sure. Lots of beaux." She smiles, acting like a flirt. I look at Dad but he's concentrating on the road.

We saw one at a football game once. He had a huge mustard overcoat and a bow tie and a pink face like a ham. He bent down to shake our tiny hands, half-looking at Mum the whole time. Dad was someplace else getting the tickets. His name was Hank. After he went, Mum put her sunglasses on her head and told us she used to watch him play football at

BC. Dad never wears a tie except to work. One time Gus got lost. We waited until the last people had trickled out and the stadium was practically empty. It had started to get dark and the headlights were crisscrossing out of the parking field. Finally Dad came back carrying him, walking fast, Gus's head bobbing around and his face all blotchy. Dad rolled his eyes and made a kidding groan to Mum and we laughed because Gus was always getting lost. When Mum took him, he rammed his head onto her shoulder and hid his face while we walked back to the car, and under Mum's hand you could see his back twitching, trying to hide his crying.

We have Ice House Pond all to ourselves. In certain places the ice is bumpy and if you glide on it going *Aauuuuhhhh* in a low tone, your voice wobbles and vibrates. Every once in a while, a crack shoots across the pond, echoing just beneath the surface, and you feel something drop in the hollow of your back. It sounds like someone's jumped off a steel wire and left it twanging in the air.

I try to teach Delilah how to skate backwards but she's flopping all over the ice, making me laugh, with her hat lopsided and her mittens dangling on strings out of her sleeves. When Gus falls, he just stays there, polishing the ice with his mitten. Dad sees him and says, "I don't care if my son is a violin player," kidding.

Dad played hockey in college and was so good his name is on a plaque that's right as you walk into the Harvard rink. He can go really fast. He takes off— *whoosh*—whizzing, circling at the edge of the pond, taking long strides, then gliding, chopping his skates, crossing over in little jumps. He goes zipping by and we watch him: his hands behind him in a tight clasp, his face as calm as if he were just walking along, only slightly forward. When he sweeps a corner, he tips in, then rolls into a hunch, and starts the long side-pushing again. After he stops, his face is red and the tears leak from the sides of his eyes and there's a white smudge around his mouth like frostbite. Sherman, copying, goes chopping forward on collapsed ankles and it sounds like someone sharpening knives.

Mum practices her 3s from when she used to figure skate. She pushes forward on one skate, turning in the middle like a petal flipped suddenly in the wind. We always make her do a spin. First she does backward crossovers, holding her wrists like a tulip in her fluorescent pink parka, then stops straight up on her toes, sucking in her breath and dips, twisted, following her own tight circle, faster and faster, drawing her feet together. Whirring around, she lowers into a crouch, ventures out one balanced leg, a twirling whirlpool, hot pink, rises again, spinning, into a blurred pillar or a tornado, her arms going above her head and her hands like the eye of a needle. Then suddenly: stop. Hiss of ice shavings, stopped. We clap our mittens. Her hood has slipped off and her hair is spread across her shoulders like when she's reading in bed, and she takes white breaths with her teeth showing and her pink mouth smiling. She squints over our heads. Dad is way off at the car, unlacing his skates on the tailgate but he doesn't turn. Mum's face means that it's time to go.

Chicky stands in the front seat leaning against Dad. Our parkas crinkle in the cold car. Sherman has been chewing on his thumb and it's a pointed black witch's hat. A rumble goes through the car like a monster growl and before we back up Dad lifts Chicky and sets him leaning against Mum instead.

The speed bumps are marked with yellow stripes and it's like sea serpents have crawled under the tar. When we bounce, Mum says, "Thank-you-ma'am" with a lilt in her voice. If it was only Mum, the radio would be on and she'd turn it up on the good ones. Dad snaps it off because there's enough racket already. He used to listen to opera when he got home from work but not anymore. Now we give him hard hugs and he changes upstairs then goes into the TV room to the same place on the couch, propping his book on his crossed knees and reaching for his drink without looking up. At supper, he comes in for a handful of onion-flavored bacon crisps or a dish of miniature corn-on-the-cobs pickled. Mum keeps us in the kitchen longer so he can have a little peace and quiet. Ask him what he wants for Christmas and he'll say, "No more arguing." When Mum clears our plates, she takes a bite of someone's hot dog or a quick spoonful of peas before dumping the rest down the pig.

In the car, we ask Dad if we can stop at Shucker's for candy. When he doesn't answer, it means *No*. Mum's eyes mean *Not today*. She says, "It's treat night anyway." Treats are ginger ale and vanilla ice cream.

On Sunday nights we have treats and BLTs and get to watch Ted Mack and Ed Sullivan. There are circus people on almost every time, doing cartwheels or flips or balancing. We stand up in our socks and try some of it. Delilah does an imitation of Elvis by making jump-rope handles into a microphone. Girls come on with silver shoes and their stomachs showing and do clappity tap dances. "That's a cinch," says Mum behind us.

"Let's see you then," we say and she goes over to the brick in front of the fireplace to show us. She bangs the floor with her sneakers, pumping and kicking, thudding her heels in smacks, not like clicking at all, swinging her arms out in front of her like she's wading through the jungle. She speeds up, staring straight at Dad who's reading his book, making us laugh even harder. He's always like that. Sometimes for no reason, he'll snap out of it, going, "What? What? What's all this? What's going on?" as if he's emerged from a dark tunnel, looking like he does when we wake him up and he hasn't put on his glasses yet, sort of angry. He sits there before dinner, popping black olives into his mouth one at a time, eyes never leaving his book. His huge glass mug is from college and in the lamplight you can see the liquid separate. One layer is beer, the rest is gin. Even smelling it makes you gag.

Dad would never take us to Shucker's for candy. With him, we do things outside. If there's a storm we go down to the rocks to see the waves—you have to yell—and get sopped. Or if Mum needs a nap, we go to the beach. In the spring it's wild and windy as anything, which I love. The wind presses against you and you kind of choke but in a good way. Sherman and I run, run, run! Couples at the end are so far away you can hardly tell they're moving. Rummy races around with other dogs, flipping his rear like a goldfish, snapping at the air, or careening in big looping circles across the beach. Caitlin jabs a stick into the wet part and draws flowers. Chicky smells the seaweed by smushing it all over his face. Delilah's dark bangs jitter across her forehead like magnets and she yells back to Gus lagging behind. Dad looks at things far away. He points out birds—a great blue heron near the breakers as thin as a safety pin or an osprey in the sky, tilting like a paper cutout. We collect little things. Delilah holds out a razor shell on one sandy palm for Dad to take and he says "Uh-huh" and calls Rummy. When Sherman, grinning, carries a dead seagull to him, Dad says, "Cut that out." Once in Maine, I found a triangle of blue and white china and showed it to Dad. "Ah yes, a bit of crockery," he said.

"Do you think it's from the Indians?" I whispered. They had made the arrowheads we found on the beach.

"I think it's probably debris," he said and handed it back to me. According to Mum, debris is the same thing as litter, as in Don't Be a Litterbug.

When we get home from skating, it's already started to get dark. Sherman runs up first and beats us to the door but can't open it himself. We are all used to how warm it was in the car so everybody's going "Brrrr," or "Hurry up," banging our feet on the porch so it thunders. The sky is dark blue glass and the railing seems whiter and the fur on Mum's hood glows. From the driveway Dad yells, "I'm going downtown. Be right back," slamming the door and starting the car again.

Delilah yells, "Can I come?" and Gus goes, "Me too!" as we watch the car back up.

"Right back," says his deep voice through the

crack in the window and he rounds the side of the house.

"How come he didn't stop on the way home?" asks Caitlin, sticking out her chin.

"Yah," says Delilah. "How come?" We look at Mum.

She kicks the door with her boot. "In we go, totsies," she says instead of answering and drops someone's skate on the porch because she's carrying so much stuff.

Gus gets in a bad mood, standing by the door with his coat on, not moving a muscle. His hat has flaps over the ears. Delilah flops onto the hall sofa, her neck bent, ramming her chin into her chest. "Why don't you take off your coat and stay awhile?" she says, drumming her fingers on her stomach as slow as a spider.

"I don't have to."

"Yah," Sherman butts in. "Who says you're the boss?" He's lying on the marble tile with Rummy, scissor-kicking his legs like windshield wipers.

"No one," says Delilah, her fingers rippling along.

On the piano bench, Caitlin is picking at her split ends. We can hear Mum in the kitchen putting the dishes away.

Banging on the piano fast because she knows it by heart, Caitlin plays "Walking in a Winter Wonderland." Delilah sits up and imitates her behind her

14

back, shifting her hips from side to side, making us all laugh. Caitlin whips around. "What?"

"Nothing." But we can't help laughing.

"Nothing what?" says Mum coming around the corner, picking up mittens and socks from the floor, snapping on the lights.

Delilah stiffens her legs. "We weren't doing anything," she says.

We make room for Mum on the couch and huddle. Gus perches at the edge, sideways.

"When's Dad coming back?" he says.

"You know your father," says Mum vaguely, smoothing Delilah's hair on her lap, daydreaming at the floor but thinking about something. When Dad goes to the store, he only gets one thing, like a can of black bean soup or watermelon rind.

"What shall we play?" says Sherman, strangling Rummy in a hug.

"Yah. Yah. Let's do something," we say and turn to Mum.

She narrows her eyes into spying slits. "All rightee. I might have a little idea."

"What?" we all shout, excited. "What?" Mum hardly ever plays with us because she has to do everything else.

She rises, slowly, lifting her eyebrows, hinting. "You'll see."

"What?" says Gus and his bottom lip loosens nervously.

Delilah's dark eyes flash like jumping beans. "Yah, Mum. What?"

"Just come with me," says Mum in a singsong and we scamper after her. At the bottom of the stairs, she crouches in the middle of us. Upstairs behind her, it's dark.

"Where are we going?" asks Caitlin, and everybody watches Mum's face, thinking of the darkness up there.

"Hee hee hee," she says in her witch voice. "We're going to surprise your father, play a little trick."

"What?" asks Caitlin again, getting ready to worry, but Mum's already creeping up the stairs so we follow, going one mile per hour like her, not making a peep even though there's no one in the house to hear us.

Suddenly she wheels around. "We're going to hide," she cackles.

"Where?" we all want to know, sneaking along like burglars.

Her voice is hushed. "Just come with me."

At the top of the stairs it is dark and we whisper.

"How about your room?" says Delilah. "Maybe under the bed."

"No," says Sherman breathlessly. "In the fireplace." We all laugh because we could never fit in there.

16

Standing in the hall, Mum opens the door to the linen closet and pulls the light-string. "How about right here?" The light falls across our faces. On the shelves are stacks of bedcovers and rolled puffs, red and white striped sheets and pink towels, everything clean and folded and smelling of soap.

All of a sudden Caitlin gasps, "Wait— I hear the car!"

Quickly we all jumble and scramble around, bumbling and knocking and trying to cram ourselves inside. Sherman makes whimpering noises like an excited dog. "Ssshhh," we say or "Hurry, Hurry," or "Wait." I knee up to a top shelf and Sherman gets a boost after me and then Delilah comes grunting up. We play in here sometimes. Gus and Chicky crawl into the shelf underneath, wedging themselves in sideways. Caitlin half-sits on molding with her legs dangling and one hand braced against the doorframe. When the rushing settles, Mum pulls out the light and hikes herself up on the other ledge. Everyone is off the ground then, and quiet.

Delilah giggles. Caitlin says "Ssshhh" and I say "Come on" in a whisper. Only when Mum says "Hush" do we all stop and listen. Everyone is breathing; a shelf creaks. Chicky knocks a towel off and it hits the ground like a pillow. Gus says, "I don't hear anything." "Ssshhh," we say. Mum touches the door and light widens and we listen. Nothing.

"False alarm," says Sherman.

17

Our eyes start to get used to the dark. Next to me Delilah gurgles her spit.

"What do you think he'll do?" whispers Caitlin. We all smile, curled up in the darkness with Mum, thinking how fooled he'll be, coming back and not a soul anywhere, standing in the hall with all the lights glaring not hearing a sound.

"Where will he think we've gone?" We picture him looking around for a long time, till finally we all pour out of the closet.

"He'll find out," Mum whispers. Someone laughs at the back of his throat, like a cricket quietly ticking.

Delilah hisses, "Wait—"

"Forget it," says Caitlin, who knows it's a false alarm.

"What will he do?" we ask Mum.

She's in the darkest part of the closet, on the other side of the light slant. We hear her voice. "We'll see."

"My foot's completely fallen asleep," says Caitlin.

"Kick it," says Mum's voice.

"Ssshhh," lisps Chicky, and we laugh at him copying everybody.

Gus's muffled voice comes from under the shelf. "My head's getting squished."

"Move it," says Delilah.

"Quiet!"

And then we really do hear the car.

18

"Silence, monkeys," says Mum, and we all hush, holding our breaths. The car hums up the hill.

The motor dies and the car shuts off. We hear the door crack, then clip shut. Footsteps bang up the echoing porch, loud, toe-hard and scuffing. The glass panes rattle when the door opens, resounding in the empty hall, and then the door slams in the dead quiet, reverberating through the whole side of the house. Someone in the closet squeaks like a hamster. Downstairs there isn't a sound.

"Anybody home?" he bellows, and we try not to giggle.

Now what will he do? He strides across the deep hall, going by the foot of the stairs, obviously wondering where everybody's gone, stopping at the hooks to hang up his parka.

"What's he doing?" whispers Caitlin to herself.

"He's by the mitten basket," says Sherman. We all have smiles, our teeth like watermelon wedges, grinning in the dark.

He yells toward the kitchen, "Hello?" and we hunch our shoulders to keep from laughing, holding on to something tight like our toes or the shelf, or biting the side of our mouths.

He starts back into the hall.

"He's getting warmer," whispers Mum's voice, far away. We all wait for his footsteps on the stairs.

But he stops by the TV room doorway. We hear

19

him rustling something, a paper bag, taking out what he's bought, the bag crinkling, setting something down on the hall table, then crumpling up the bag and pitching it in the wastebasket. Gus says, "Why doesn't he—?" "Ssshhh," says Mum like spitting and we all freeze. He moves again—his footsteps turn and bang on the hollow threshold into the TV room where the rug pads the sound.

Next we hear the TV click on, the sound swelling and the dial switching *tick-ah tikka tikka tick* till it lands on a crowd roar, a football game. We can hear the announcer's voice and the hiss-breath behind it of cheering.

Then it's the only sound in the house.

"What do we do now?" says Delilah only half-whispering. Mum slips down from her shelf and her legs appear in the light, touching down.

Still hushed, Sherman goes, "Let's keep hiding."

The loud thud is from Caitlin jumping down. She uses her regular voice. "Forget it. I'm sick of this anyway." Everyone starts to rustle. Chicky panics, "I can't get down," as if we're about to desert him.

"Stop being such a baby," says Delilah, disgusted.

Mum doesn't say anything, just opens the door all the way. Past the banister in the hall it is yellow and bright. We climb out of the closet, feet-feeling our way down backward, bumping out one at a time, knocking down blankets and washcloths by mistake.

20

Mum guides our backs and checks our landings. We don't leave the narrow hallway. The light from downstairs shines up through the railing and casts shadows on the wall—bars of light and dark like a fence. Standing in it we have stripes all over us. "Hey look," we say whispering, with the football drone in the background, even though this isn't anything new— we always see this, holding out your arms and seeing the stripes. Lingering near the linen closet, we wait. Mum picks up the tumbled things, restacking the stuff we knocked down, folding things, clinching a towel with her chin, smoothing it over her stomach and then matching the corners left and right, like crossing herself, patting everything into neat piles. The light gets like this every night after we've gone to bed and we creep into the hall to listen to Mum and Dad downstairs. The bands of shadows go across our nightgowns and pajamas and we press our foreheads against the railing trying to hear the mumbling of what Mum and Dad are saying down there. Then we hear the deep boom of Dad clearing his throat and look up at Mum. Though she is turned away, we still can see the wince on her face like when you are waiting to be hit or right after you have been. So we keep standing there, our hearts pounding, waving our hands through the flickered stripes, suddenly interested the way you get when it's time to take a bath and you are mesmerized by something.

We're stalling, waiting for Mum to finish folding, waiting to see what she's going to do next because we don't want to go downstairs yet, where Dad is, without her.

THANKSGIVING DAY

Gus and Rosie Vincent waited for their six children to crawl out of the station wagon and then slammed the doors. The Vincents were always the first to arrive.

They would pull up to the house in Motley, Massachusetts, where their father grew up, and crunch across the gravel, and in the doorway was Ma with her dark blue dress pleated from collar to waist and they would give her kisses, then file in to dump their coats in the coatroom and right away the first thing would be the smell of Pa's cigar. He waited in the other room. Every Thanksgiving they descended upon him and every year it was the same.

The three girls wore matching plaid skirts with plaid suspender straps. Caitlin and Sophie, who looked alike, had on hair bands of the same material. Delilah, the youngest daughter, was darker, with a short pixie. She said it wasn't fair she didn't get to have long hair too. The three boys came after, Gus and Sherman and Chicky, in gray flannels. Chicky's were shorts, since he was the baby.

For Sophie, the best thing was getting to see the cousins, especially the other Vincents. Bit, the only girl cousin, was Sophie's age, eleven. And Churly was the oldest of everybody; he was fourteen. Churly and Bit arrived with Uncle Charles and Aunt Ginny. Sophie hesitated because sometimes you didn't give them a kiss. On Aunt Ginny's cardigan was the turkey pin she wore every year. The other cousins were the Smalls. Aunt Fran used to be a Vincent before she married Uncle Thomas. They had three boys. The oldest was Teever Small, who drooled.

Once everyone was there, the children had to put their coats back on for the annual picture. Bit had a white rabbit muff that Teever Small grabbed at, trying to flirt. "That's enough of that," said his father, but Bit had already snatched it back. Sophie felt how soft the fur was, thinking about the dead rabbit; the muff was in the shape of a rabbit too. The grown-ups shuffled everybody around, then stood beside Sophie's father, who had the camera. They crossed

24

their arms against the cold, talking to one another and watching to make sure the kids didn't move.

"I'll be doggone," said Uncle Thomas. Sophie stared at his bow tie. "Will you look at that."

"A bunch of young ladies and young gentlemen," said Aunt Fran, smacking her orange lips. She had white hair like Ma's, except hers was short.

"Knock it off, Churly," Uncle Charles said.

Sophie turned around. Churly was smirking. He had a head shaped like a wooden golf club, with his long neck, and a crew cut like the other boys. Sophie looked back at the house and saw Ma inside, watching through the French doors.

After the picture was taken, Rosie Vincent told her children to say hello to Livia, and the cousins tagged along. The hall to the kitchen was dark, the floor with a sheen from the glow at the end. The kitchen was pale gray, with no lights on and a white enamel table in the middle. Livia gave them pinched kisses, her eyes darting around the room, checking on food, on the children. She was huge and huffing in her white uniform. The kitchen smelled of Worcestershire sauce and turkey. "Are you behaving yourselves now?" She held up a shiny wooden spoon. When she was cooking, everything on Livia sweated, the steam rising behind her from the pots on the stove.

"Not me," Churly said. "I always try to be as naughty as possible."

Caitlin laughed while Sophie looked at Livia's face, which meant business. Livia sat down. "Now what are the seven blessed sacraments?" she asked, addressing Gus and Rosie's children—Catholic, thanks to their mother. Livia tipped one ear forward the way Sophie had seen the priest do in confession. Sophie fingered a tin Jell-O mold shaped like a fish, and Caitlin busied herself by tucking in Sherman's shirttails. No one answered. Livia rattled them off herself, slicing apples so the blade came right to her thumb without even looking. The cousins drifted off into the pantry as Livia thought up new questions— all having to do with catechism.

The dining-room table had already been set. The cranberry sauce had a spoon sticking out. Bit stole some mint wafers, reaching past the blue water goblets into the middle of the table, and gave one to Sophie. "It's okay," said Bit, noticing Sophie's expression.

"I saw that," Churly said from the doorway. Sophie blushed. He came in and whispered, "All right, you guys . . ." and she saw how his eyes were like those light blue paperweights that had white lines of glass streaked from the middle. He leaned past them and plucked a candy out of the cut-glass boat. "Delish," he said. "Don't mind if I do."

In the living room, the grown-ups stood stirring drinks at the red-leather bar stand; then they sat down. Sophie's mother was the only one without a scotch or a Dubonnet. There was nothing to do while the grown-ups talked except to look around at each tiny thing. Three walls were covered with books, and over the mantelpiece was a portrait of Dr. Vincent, so dark and shiny that the lights reflected off it. One side of the room was all French windows, with dead vines at the edges. The windows overlooked the lawn. Beside the fireplace was a child's rocking chair with a red back, an antique. Gus had gotten to it first and was sitting there, holding on to his ankles, next to Ma's place on the sofa. They had the hard kind of sofas with wooden arms and wood in a curve along the back. You could tell it was Ma's place because of the brown smudge on the ceiling from her cigarette smoke.

The girls examined their grandmother. Her shoes, the pair her granddaughters liked the best, were pale lavender with pink trim and flat bows, her fancy shoes.

"Gussie," said Aunt Fran, the one person in the world who called Sophie's father that. She said it as if it tasted bad. "How'd you like the game?" The last time they had seen each other was at the Harvard halftime in October when they were stretching their legs under the bleachers. Gus, with his children, said,

"Good day to you," as if he saw his sister every day, which he didn't, each walking in the opposite direction.

The grown-ups talked about the sports the boys were playing.

"Churly's on the debating team," said Uncle Charles.

"I certainly am," said Churly, the only one of the children taking up a seat. "Anyone want to argue?"

Under a lamp was a picture of Ma before she married. She was holding a plume of roses at her waist, her chin to the side, her dark eyes and dark hair swept up.

The grown-ups were talking about the woman next door who died after she cut her finger on a splinter from a Christmas-tree ornament. Ma said how appropriate it was that a pheasant appeared out of the woods at Mr. Granger's funeral.

"But *she* was the one who loved to shoot," said Aunt Fran with her Adam's apple thrust out.

"Terrible story about their son," said Sophie's mother. Her thumb rubbed her knuckle while the conversation continued.

They talked without looking at each other, their chairs all facing in. Aunt Fran addressed her remarks to the one spot in the room where no one sat or stood. She and Uncle Thomas were having a pond dug in the back of their house and by mistake the

28

workers had struck a pipe. Aunt Fran and Uncle Thomas told the story at the same time, interrupting each other.

Uncle Charles said, "It's like a zoo at my house." When he made jokes, he barely cracked a smile. Bit was lucky, she got to have a pony and three dogs and sheep. "Our sheep just stand there in the rain," said Churly.

Uncle Charles said the chickens hated him. And now they had a turtle, with a chain attached to the loop on its shell so it wouldn't run away. "It chooses to sleep where I'm accustomed to park my car," he said.

"A what?" said Pa, angry at having to strain.

"Turtle," yelled Uncle Charles.

"Where's our turtle soup then?" Pa said, and some of the family chuckled. Sophie didn't think he was kidding. He sat there still as a statue, his hands gripping the mahogany claws of his chair.

Sophie and Delilah hovered near their mother. Delilah whispered, "Can we go look at the lion yet?"

Rosie Vincent patted her daughter's back till Aunt Ginny finished describing the flower show at the armory. Then she said, "Ask your grandfather."

Delilah and Sophie didn't care about going right that second, so they crossed the room to the shadow box wedged in between the books. Behind the glass was a scene with an island and a beach and pine trees. The rowboat in the water was as big as a little shack stuck with lobster pots. They heard their mother call, "Did you ask him?" The girls turned around, closemouthed. Rosie Vincent said to Pa, "The children want to go look at the lion."

Pa's head was lowered. He was staring at them from across the room, his chin slack. "Watch out it doesn't bite you," he snapped.

Out in the hall, Gus said he wasn't coming. Churly told him, "It's okay, I'll fight him off." Caitlin came out once she saw Churly was going along.

The lion was in the attic. On the second floor were bedrooms, and on the third floor the attic. Everyone clumped up the stairs. The attic hall was swept clean, no rugs or furniture in the rooms on one side, just the thin light coming in the windows and a dry cedar smell. One room was filled—trunks with wooden slats and, on shelves, newspaper clippings and tied-up letters and pink-striped hatboxes, and Brooks Brothers boxes with old army uniforms in them. The yellow tweed suitcases looked shellacked.

They crept into the big room at the end of the hall. It had slanted ceilings and high windows. Behind them, Churly screeched and everyone screamed and grabbed each other and laughed. In a glass case were seashells furry with dust and, in some trunks, silverware rolled up in felt or candlesticks that fit into the blue velvet cases like chess pieces. The lion lay in the middle of the floor, splayed out flat as a pancake except for its great head. Ma's father had shot it on safari. Its mouth was raised up in a roar, the nostrils wrinkled and two sharp teeth coming down on either side. The pink tongue was made out of fired clay, glazed. Bit was the only one who dared to touch it. It rattled in the hard mouth. The top of the lion's head was almost bald from being touched, or from being old. Sophie lay down and put her cheek next to the ears, knowing they were the softest part.

Caitlin sat next to Churly at the bar, pouring a ginger ale. Sophie got Bit and Delilah to go to the owl room, and the boys followed. There were glass owls and a hollow brass owl with a hinge so its head lifted off, two china owls with flowers, owl engravings, and a needlepoint of an owl that Caitlin had done from a kit. They had a game they played by closing their eyes and then going nose to nose with someone and saying "One, two, three, *Owl-lee, Owl-lee*" and opening their eyes, imitating an owl. Delilah and Sherman were playing it.

Stretching down the corridor were group silhouettes of Vincent ancestors, black cutouts of children with ringlets, holding hoops, or men with bearded profiles. There were Pa's team pictures from Noble & Greenough and his class pictures

31

from Harvard. All the faces in the photographs had straight noses and white eyeballs and hide-gray complexions. In one, Pa lay on his side, lengthwise, in front of everyone else. Sophie tried to match him with the Pa back in the living room. You never saw Pa smile, that was common knowledge, except in one picture the Vincents had at home, of Pa with the Senator. His job had been to write speeches, and, according to Sophie's mother, he got a dollar a year to do it. In the picture, his grin is closed, like a clown's. There was Pa in an army uniform—but Sophie knew the story of that. Pa missed the war, sailing to France on the exact day armistice was declared. At the end of the hall, Sophie came to the picture of Pa's brother, the famous doctor who discovered the cure for a disease whose name she could never remember. He had died a long time ago.

When they drifted back into the living room, Uncle Charles was recalling when the lawn froze and they could skate over the sunken garden.

"Not true," said Pa, gurgling. "My lawn was never an ice rink."

"Sure," said Sophie's father. "Everything was frozen solid."

Pa said, "Never happened in my lifetime."

Uncle Charles clamped on his pipe with his back teeth. "Oh yes it did, Pa. You must be losing your memory." His voice was squeaky.

"Ma," demanded Pa.

With her perfectly calm face, Ma said, "I do remember it, yes." She looked at Pa and said gently, "It was when you were away."

"Nonsense," he said. "I never went anywhere."

The children's table was wobbly. This year Sophie got to sit at the big table, and Caitlin and Churly, too. Bit said she was glad to stay at the children's table where she wouldn't have to use good manners.

When the plates came, they had everything on them already, even creamed onions whether you liked them or not. Pa looked down at the food in front of him.

"Gravy, Granpa?" shouted Aunt Fran. Half-frowning, he regarded her. She swung a silver ladle over his turkey, bringing it up with a flourish. "Yummy," she said in a booming voice.

Everyone at the table used loud voices—family behavior. When Sophie went out to go to the bathroom, she stood in the hall for a moment between the Chinese portraits and listened to the clatter behind her, the hollow echo from the high ceilings, Aunt Fran's hooting, the knives clicking on the china, her mother's voice saying something quietly to the little table. Sophie could tell Uncle Charles from his whine, and her grandmother was the slow voice

enunciating each word the way old people do because they're tired of talking. Sophie went up close
to study one Indian picture—you could see the
tongue of the snake and the man's pink fingernails
and even the horse's white eyelashes. Ma said they
used one cat hair at a time to paint it. In the bathroom was the same brown soap shaped like an owl.
The towels she used were so stiff it was like drying
your hands with paper.

Sophie came back as Aunt Fran was saying, "He's a
crook."

"Now stop that," said Ma, lifting her chin.

"Who is?" asked Churly, brightening.

"Never mind," said Ma to her knife and fork.

So Churly asked, "What'd he steal?"

Ma said, "They've started reshingling the house in
North Eden." The Vincents went to Maine every
summer. A drawer in one of the side tables was
always kept pulled out—a red velvet slab with rows
of arrowheads, ones that Pa had found on Boxed
Island in Maine. You played kick-the-can on the slop-
ing lawn after supper. When Churly was it, Sophie
would let herself get caught. One time, playing spy,
they saw Ma on her balcony with her hair all down,
falling down her arms like a white shawl. Sometimes
Ma and Pa were like ghosts. You'd see them pass

behind a window in their house, or snapping out a light and vanishing. In the daytime, Ma's hair was twisted into a knot at the back.

Aunt Fran was wondering whether there didn't used to be a porch around the house out at Cassett Harbor, the old house. Uncle Thomas shouted, "That's right. Mrs. Lothrop said they'd have the Herreshoff teas on that porch."

"The correct term," said Ma, "is piazza."

"It must have been quite a view," said Sophie's mother.

"It's where you'd sit with your beaux," said Ma.

"We tore down the piazza," said Pa. Sophie was surprised he was listening.

Aunt Fran said, "I thought it burned down."

"Yes." Ma's nod was meant to end the discussion.

"How'd it burn down?" Churly asked. His long neck went up and his ears stuck out. Sophie felt herself flushing.

Pa said, "It—was—torn—down." His shoulders were round and low and his chin hovered inches above his plate.

Down at her end, Ma said, "The remainder was torn down, yes." Pa glared at her. His bottom lip drooped, as white as the rest of his face.

"How'd it burn down?" Churly asked eagerly.

Ma pulled some empty dishes over the tablecloth toward her. "You finish," she said. She stood up and

35

carried some things to the sideboard, then glanced over the table to see what else to take. She piled small dishes on the turkey platter in front of Pa and went to lift it.

"Don't touch that," he said. He didn't look at her, or at the platter, but stared at the middle of the table.

"I think you're done," said his wife.

Sophie's mother pushed her chair back. "Let me. . . ." Her napkin bloomed like a white flower when she let go of it on the table.

"I'm not through," said Pa. "I want to pick." He didn't move.

"Now, Pa," said Aunt Fran. "We've got Livia's pies coming."

"Damn Livia's pies," he said. "Only occasionally you will disguise a voyage and cancel all that crap."

The little table fell quiet.

"I'm all ready for dessert." Uncle Thomas looked perky. "You ready for dessert there, Churly?"

Churly nodded, then looked to see what Pa would do next.

Caitlin and Sophie started to take their plates, but their mother gave them a stay-put look and made several quick trips through the swinging door.

Pa growled, "I've been eating goddamn custard all Monday."

Aunt Ginny asked, "What kind of pies do we have?" Each year they had the same: apple, mince, and pumpkin. Everyone began saying which kind they wanted. Ma sat back down.

As they ate their pie and ice cream, Pa kept mumbling. "Bunch of idiots. . . . Going to knock it off like a bullhorn. . . . Newspaper, *then* cigar. . . ."

"No dessert for you, Pa?" Uncle Charles asked.

"I wouldn't set foot in there to piss," said Pa Vincent.

Ma went down and whispered into Pa's ear. No one could hear what she said, but Pa answered in a loud, slow voice, "Why don't you go shoot yourself?"

In the kitchen, Sophie and Caitlin watched Churly tell Livia. She fidgeted with pans and finally set them in the sink. "Your grandfather just needs his nap," said Livia. She studied the children's faces to see if they understood this. She was frowning. Her gaze drifted off and she turned her mammoth back to them, kept on sudsing things in the sink. She muttered, "He'll be wanting his . . ." but they couldn't hear what.

In the living room, the grown-ups were serving coffee. On the tray were miniature blue enamel cups, a silver bowl holding light-brown-sugar rocks, and chocolate mints in tissue-paper envelopes.

Ma and Aunt Fran came down from upstairs where they had taken Pa.

37

"Everything all right?" bellowed Uncle Thomas. His wife scowled at him.

Ma took her place on the sofa. "Fine," she said. "Fine."

Rosie handed her a cup with a tiny gold spoon placed on the saucer. Delilah, her arm draped across her mother's knee, felt brave. "Was Pa mad at us?" she asked. Caitlin glared at her.

"Hah," shouted Uncle Charles, half-laughing, "he wasn't mad at me."

Sophie's father said, "He didn't know what he was saying, Delou." He was over by the window.

Ma sipped at the rim of her cup. Gus Vincent touched the curtain with one finger and gazed out. Rosie busily poured more coffee.

Looking at Delilah, Ma said, "He was not mad at you, dear."

Aunt Ginny looked up, surprised. "The turkey was delicious," she said.

"Oh shut up, Virginia," said Uncle Charles.

Sophie looked at Churly and noticed his ears sticking out and all his features flattened out, stiff, into a mask.

Uncle Thomas said, "Super meal, super." He jiggled the change in his pocket, waiting for something to happen.

"You can thank Livia for that." Ma set down her saucer. Sherman was in the rocking chair at her feet, lurching to and fro.

"Yes," said Rosie Vincent, "but you arranged it so beautifully."

Ma folded her hands. Her expression was matter-of-fact. "Actually, I don't think I've ever arranged anything beautifully in my whole life."

The grown-ups exchanged looks and for a moment there was no sound except for Sherman creaking in the rocking chair at Ma's feet. He got up, all at once aware of himself, and scurried to his mother. The chair went on rocking. Ma stared at it. Rocking empty, it meant something to her.

So she reached out one lavender shoe to still it, and did just that.

ALLOWANCE

Of the six Vincent children trapped inside Colonus Cottage at the Pearl Bay Hotel in Bermuda, Gus, aged ten, was displaying the most extreme signs of cabin fever. He snapped a towel at the lampshade, at the wastebasket with the soldiers marching across it, at his younger brother Sherman. Sherman, who was on the floor playing the millionth game of Go Fish with Chicky, told Gus to quit it, but Gus didn't stop, and finally Caitlin, writing postcards at the breakfast table, said, "Gus, I'm warning you," without looking up, which caused Gus to slink to the other side of the room where he flicked at a pillow, furtively, and then glanced back at Caitlin. She was scribbling, her mouth was set. Behind her, the rain, which had not stopped all day, drummed down on a metal table out on the terrace. Gus turned away and cuffed the back of a wicker chair.

"You're giving me a mental heart attack," Delilah said. She had her leg draped over an armrest and was bobbing it around.

"What am I doing?" Gus said.

"Just everything," Delilah said. She shook a brittle seedpod and examined it with boredom.

"You're acting like you need a lobotomy," Sophie said. The book in her lap was open, but she was not reading.

"What's a lobotomy?" Sherman asked. He had on his Roman-gladiator shield, which helped fight off the dragons at naptime.

"It's when they cut out part of your brain and turn you into a vegetable."

"Gross," Caitlin said. She was fourteen, the oldest.

"For some mental cases it's the only thing that makes them calm down," Sophie said straight to Gus.

"What am I doing?" Gus said. Gus was usually the quietest one, drinking his milk at supper while everyone else tried to monopolize the conversation. When they put on plays, the girls took over the main parts —the queen, the princess, the witch—and Gus would be the guard or the messenger or the guy who

42

gets killed. Sherman and Chicky, the two youngest, were the audience—one that got up and wandered away before the play was over. But since the Vincents had gotten to Bermuda, Gus had not been able to sit still. It was the first real vacation they'd been on, as opposed to going to just New Hampshire or Vermont to ski. Bermuda had been Mum's idea. Other families from Marshport, the small town in Massachusetts where they lived, had houses there that Mum wanted to see. Before, there had always been too many monkeys, but now that Chicky was five, they were manageable. Gus was the oldest boy, the first boy after three girls. He was named after Dad.

Things were different in Bermuda. The grass was scratchy and rough, not at all like the grass at home, and the air had a thickness that made your bones feel loose. Stepping into the coral caves was like entering a seashell, with a low wind rushing and the echo of water slaps. Rays wheeled by through the pleated shallows on strange rubber wings, and green lizards, like elongated stars, appeared stuck onto the white walls inside the cottage. Gus claimed he saw a hunchbacked animal on the golf course one night; it was a laughing hyena, he said, with yellow eyes and striped fur. No one but the little boys believed him.

"I think one of those ticks got into your brain," Delilah said.

"What," Gus said.

Delilah sighed. "The ticks you got, Gus."

"Mum took them off," Sherman said.

"I know," Delilah said. "But when they hatch eggs under your skin, they can get anywhere."

"Mum flushed those down the toilet," Gus said.

"That won't even kill them," Sophie said. "You have to burn them."

"Even if they were this tiny?" Sherman said. He put his fingertips together and made a little space.

"It doesn't matter their size," Sophie said.

"We *do* have ticks at home," Caitlin said.

"Well," Delilah said, "they're different from the ones here."

Gus was standing at the window. The fairway was soaked to a dark green, lined with spiky palms, ending at a cloudy smudge that was the ocean. "Lots of things are different here," he said.

"Gus already wants to go home," Delilah said.

"I do not."

"Well, he better like it here," Caitlin said. "It's costing a hundred dollars a day."

The door at the far end of the room opened and everyone stopped talking. Their mother, freckled and handsome, came out in a bathrobe—something she'd never be wearing at home.

"Mum," Caitlin said. "Tell Gus to calm down."

Mum glanced into a corner. "Where are the little

boys?" she asked vaguely. Everyone looked at her; you never saw Mum distracted quite this way.

"Right here," came Sherman's voice from behind the couch.

Mum nodded and drifted over to the mantelpiece as if trying to remember something. One of her eyebrows went up dreamily. She folded her arms. Then she remembered; she looked up. But no. . . . It was something else. . . . She frowned. Then came a weird grimace, and her skin cracked like rice paper, and she burst into tears.

Everyone froze. Delilah's leg went still. Sherman's head rose like a periscope from behind the couch.

"It's Dad," Mum said. "He—" Her eyes were shiny with visions.

Gus stepped forward. "What about him?" His bottom lip was red and eager with spit, his teeth working at it.

"He thinks—" But she couldn't go on and was overtaken by little sobs and jumpy breaths. They all waited, stunned.

"What?" Gus said.

"No," Mum said, ashamed. "It's okay. It's just things at the bank, and he thinks . . ." This hurt, and she winced.

"Do you want to go home?" Caitlin said gently. Her pen was clutched in its writing angle, her brow creased. "We can, you know."

45

Sophie and Delilah were both nodding. They knew it must be serious if Dad mentioned the bank. He never mentioned work.

Mum began a weak smile and sniffed. "No, no," she said, and looked at them fondly. It was like the end of church, when the priest says, "The Mass is ended; go in peace." They all began to stir, to help it end quickly.

Caitlin went over to her. "Don't you worry about it, love," Mum said, her voice composed and assured again. She began to rub Caitlin's back.

On the floor were towels the boys had left lying around. As Mum picked them up, Gus stole glances at the opening of her bathrobe. Straightening, she flipped back her hair in a familiar gesture—efficient, back to her usual business of cleaning up after the boys. Before going back to her and Dad's room, she turned and whispered to the children, playfully, meaning that this wasn't so serious after all. "Let's just not bother him too much," she said and wrinkled her nose.

Before dinner, the girls huddled behind the cottage, out of sight. They had gotten the cigarettes from Dad's carton, which, along with the gallon of bourbon, went with him wherever he went. The carton and the bottle sat on the bureau next to Mum's jewelry pouch—the velvet one that zipped in pearls and dangly earrings. The bottle of bourbon was even at the hospital when Dad had his appendix out; Mum had snuck it in under her raincoat.

Caitlin took a loud puff. "I *thought* Dad was acting weird this morning," she said. Sophie nodded.

"He was not," Delilah said, watching her sisters practice smoke rings. Delilah was only twelve and didn't smoke yet.

Dad had come out of his room slapping his putter like a riding crop. "Morning, all," he said. "Satisfactory breakfast?" Everyone nodded and hummed. "Want some?" Caitlin asked, holding out her muffin with marmalade on it. Dad had shaken his head quite decisively and bent over to putt. They all watched. He brought back the putter, swung it through, making a *tlock* sound with his tongue, and, with knees bent and slightly twisted, he posed as still as a statue. Around the breakfast table there was a gentle craning of necks as the invisible ball rolled over the straw carpet. When Dad unfroze, it meant the ball had stopped, so they could stop paying attention. He frowned, unhappy with the stroke. But Dad never looked satisfied with anything he did.

Above the girls, by the cottage's back door, an electric grid zapped the evening insects in a quick, blue flash. "Gus beat him yesterday at golf, you know," Sophie said.

"That's impossible," Delilah said. She pulled her dress over her knees and rocked.

"Dad doesn't like vacations anyway," Caitlin said.

"He does so," Delilah said. Dad took off two weeks each year. Mum said the bank would give him more if he asked, but he never did.

"Does it really cost that much, Caitlin?" Sophie asked.

Caitlin tapped her ash and nodded gravely. She knew about these things. Looks of concern passed over her sisters' faces: how much of the expense was solely for their benefit?

"You're always making a big deal out of everything," Delilah said.

"I am not," Caitlin said. "How would you like it—spending all your money on other people?"

"I'm not a father," Delilah said. She began brushing off a flagstone. "Besides, you're the one charging ginger ales in the game room."

"Once."

"Still." Delilah waved away some smoke making a sour face. "Anyway, why don't you use your own money?"

"I would," Caitlin said. "If Dad would just give us a regular allowance."

"He gives you money whenever you ask him," Sophie said.

"Right," Caitlin said with a knowing look. *"You ask him."*

"We're not meant to bother him," Delilah said.

Caitlin and Sophie both rolled their eyes. "Thanks, Delilah," they said. "Thanks for the information."

For dinner that night they had green soup. Dad sat at the head; they were careful not to look straight at him. They snuck glances—he had a funny expression, blinking behind his glasses, trying to stay awake.

"Is this turtle soup?" Sherman asked. They had the biggest table in the dining room, taking the same seats each night, the way they did at home.

"No," Mum said. "It's pea—even better than turtle."

"I bet I wouldn't like turtle," Sherman said.

"Everyone has to try it," Mum said.

"What if you hate peas?" Delilah said.

"Look," Mum said. "Dad likes it." It was okay to look at Dad now. He was one inch from the bowl, and his mouth was fumbling over his spoon. "Yoohoo," Mum called.

It woke him. Dad glanced around the table. Perplexed, he saw six children, six hopeful faces looking back at him. Down at the other end was a woman in a pink dress. What did they want? He stood and excused himself.

49

"Where's he going?" Gus asked.

Mum shrugged flirtatiously: that was a secret. She sipped her soup as if it were the best thing she'd ever tasted. She didn't seem to be so worried about Dad anymore.

Dad came back and sat down. He had a new drink, one with white onions rolling around at the bottom.

After the soup bowls were taken away, plates were put down with roast beef and potatoes on them. The waiter was the same waiter they'd had every night—an old man, pale, with white hair. He looked like their priest at home, Father Florie. That made it seem funny for him to be a waiter. He seemed wise.

"There's so much fat on it," Sherman said. Mum went, "Ahem."

"That's the best part," Gus said. It was what Dad always said, that it was his favorite part. Gus went along with Dad's taste, down to the radishes Dad ate before dinner. Though the way Gus chewed showed that he didn't really like them.

"I think we should all give Dad a big thank-you for the vacation," Mum said.

They did, in unison. Dad nodded abruptly. Everyone went busily to the plates.

A sound came from Dad.

"You okay?" Mum asked.

Dad pulled at his collar, frowning. A tie was something he wouldn't usually have on for dinner. "Hot in here," he muttered.

Mum said why didn't he have some water.

Dad tapped his empty glass and the waiter came over. After he poured water for Dad, he surveyed the table to make sure everyone was taken care of, smiled personally at Chicky, and went away.

Dad picked up his glass, lifted it over his head, and turned it upside down. The water came splashing off his forehead, running down and dribbling onto his shoulders. "There," he said with drops on his earlobes. "Much better."

Sherman started to smile, then saw from everyone else's face that this was not funny.

They looked at Mum. Down at her end of the table, she was doing something with her glass of water. She dipped her fingers into it as if it were holy water, but, instead of crossing herself, absentmindedly, the way she did when arriving late for church, she purposefully dabbed the water around her neck like perfume. She turned to Chicky beside her and smiled at him, hard. "Much better is right," she said, and she folded her arms, slumping down on her elbows. She sighed as if she were relieved, though she wasn't—her eyes were furious. She was refusing to look at Dad.

Caitlin said, "Something's the matter with Gus." She pushed back her chair and rushed over to him.

Gus was sitting there, not making a sound, but his face was red and getting redder, and his eyes were round and terrified. When Gus was small, he used to cry so hard he'd faint. The girls had been taught to say "Breathe, Gus, breathe" as his face darkened into purple. Eventually, he'd pass out and keel over. Mum called him Goatie, after the baby goats that fainted from fear, going stiff and falling over when you chased them. But Gus wasn't crying now.

"What's the matter?" Delilah said angrily.

"He's choking," Sophie said. Gus looked as if he'd been tattled on. His chest started to heave and a cough threatened to escape, but he stifled it.

Mum shot out of her chair and was beside him. "Spit it out," she ordered. She thumped his back. Gus kept holding whatever it was down. A huge vein appeared on his forehead.

Caitlin screamed, "Spit it out, Gus!"

"Mum's doing it," Sophie said, and tried to pull her back to her chair.

"Not very well," Caitlin said fiercely.

The table was in an uproar. Sophie said, "Gus, try coughing," and Caitlin said, "Will everybody stop yelling?" as Sherman was saying, "Why doesn't he just swallow it?"

"Because, Sherman," said Delilah, "he can't."

The waiter appeared. He hurried over to Gus and lifted him out of his chair. Taking hold of his ankles, he turned him upside down and shook him with short jerks—the kind one might use on a clogged shaker of salt or a temperamental fountain pen—and this worked.

Most of the time they spent at the beach. The boys ran around throwing balls, climbing rocks. Gus kept his eyes on the top of a driftwood stick and did spins, turning around and around. "Watch, Dad!" he cried. "Watch me!" Then he'd topple over. Dad sat behind the girls in a rickety chair he'd found on the beach, wearing sneakers and socks. "No balls in the house," he called when Caitlin got beaned by an overthrow. They lined up for pictures. "Attention!" Dad would shout, and they scurried around, arranging themselves in order: Caitlin Sophie Delilah Gus Sherman Chicky, their palms flat against their sides, chins pulled in. When Dad said, "At ease," it meant they should put one foot to the side, clasp their wrists behind their backs, and do a little sway.

Ice-cream men strolled the beach, bumping aluminum coolers against their hips. The boys met in a huddle and planned a strategy. Chicky got sent on the mission to Dad. Gus and Sherman watched Dad shift in his chair, going for his back pocket, and saw Chicky take a bill and then glance back at his brothers, waiting in the distance. Chicky said something else to Dad, and Dad handed him another bill and immediately tucked his wallet back under his seat. Chicky came running back, kicking up sand, and handed the money to Gus, who ordered for them: one Rocket, one Rainbow Delight, and a sundae cup. When the girls, flat out on their towels, started asking for bites, Gus turned to Mum with a tortured face, meaning "Can't they get their own?" Dad was already hitching into his back pocket. Sophie and Delilah took the dollars—stiff as sandpaper—asking Dad did he want something. He shook his head. A drink even? No, he didn't, thank you. Mum called out that she wouldn't mind one of those banana Popsicles. The one she'd had yesterday had really hit the spot.

They visited the fort, a plateau of leveled ruins with grass blowing and rubble. Gus wanted to know where all the men were; he had a fort at home, with cavalry. "Where indeed," Dad said, pacing off a boundary with stiff knees. "Where indeed."

"Away from the edge," Mum called casually.

Dad whipped around. Sherman was peering down the cliff, where coral islands were humped like haystacks in the sea. "Obey your mother!" Dad shouted.

To Dad, everything was dangerous. The roads

here were deathtraps, he said. They saw a lot of accidents—policemen waving traffic by, and hollow helmets lying in the road. They would have rented a car, but it wasn't worth it. Gus and the girls rode bicycles—better exercise anyway, Mum said—while Chicky and Sherman rode with Mum and Dad on their motorbikes. Serene and bug-headed in their helmets, they glided by Gus and the girls, who had to pedal furiously before every hill. "So long, suckers," Sherman said, puttering past, gloating, sitting behind Dad, whose attention remained fixed on points farther along the road.

It was on one of the last days that Dad's wallet disappeared. "Attention, everybody," Mum said. "Major hunt."

"Where'd he have it last?" Sophie asked. Dad was in his room with the door shut.

"Can't remember," Mum said. She was down on her hands and knees, checking under a bamboo bookshelf.

Caitlin, who had her towel and her bag, all ready for the beach, said, "Maybe it got stolen."

"Everybody look," Mum said. Sometimes there were rewards; you found Mum's scissors or the missing glove and got a reward for it.

"Just say a prayer to Saint Anthony," Delilah said. This always worked for her.

They searched about listlessly, picking up cushions and dropping them, opening drawers with nothing inside. The boys tripped out onto the terrace, pushing each other, and when Sherman and Chicky came back in, they gave huge sighs. The search would never end.

Then they heard a cry from outside. Everyone turned to see Gus appear in the doorway, his face showing wavering surprise. His palm was thrust forward, lifted up, and on it he had the wallet. "I found it in the bushes," he said uncertainly.

Mum watched him. "Yes," she said. "Here." Gus stared at the wallet, not at Mum, as she took it. When Dad came out of his room, the whole family was assembled.

"The Goatie came up with it," Mum said.

Dad took the wallet and opened it. It was brown leather, warped in the shape of his back pocket. He began to go through the bills, separating them one at a time with his thumb. He had a funny expression, Dad did, his eyebrows with that lift you see on people who have been hypnotized, or on daydreamers.

"So everything's okay?" Gus said. Mum was plumping some pillows, holding her chin the way she did when someone was about to take her picture, composing herself. "Do I get a reward?" he asked. Dad didn't respond. Gus tried to smile and, swaggering, turned toward his brothers and sisters. All their eyes were on him, and all watched his expression change, withering into panic, as if he thought that at any moment they would pounce on him.

It wasn't that. They just knew what he'd done.

WILDFLOWERS

"Maybe we should help her," said Sophie, sitting on the window seat of the front room. The open windows let in the luffing of sails and the clanging of halyards, but louder than that were dishes, making a clatter in the kitchen.

"She hasn't asked," said Caitlin with a smile. Their feet, barely touching, did not move. Out in the harbor sailboats were circling one another, tacking this way and that, positioning themselves before the starting gun. Kids in rowboats shot jackknife sprays with their oars while other kids watched from railings above. Mum passed by the living room and out the door. Sophie and Caitlin heard her squeal in the wind and rolled their eyes. She reappeared on the dock carrying a plate of brownies in one hand and a vase of flowers in the other. Her dress fluttered about her, the vase bent back like a torch. It was part of it for the ladies giving the Saturday race teas to bring flowers, usually from their own gardens—careful arrangements of dahlias and zinnias and sweet william. Mum had brought wildflowers—loosestrife and buttercups and queen anne's lace. There was no space for a garden at the Vincents', with the dock in front and Main Street just up the steps—the vegetable garden was in another place entirely—so Mum gathered flowers up island. She found fields everywhere shimmering down to the sea, flowers scattered and random, not boxed inside walls. On her bedside table she kept a small vase, always fresh.

"She's feeling her oats," Sophie said, watching Mum head for the clubhouse at the end of the dock. Inside the mahogany darkness, other bright dresses were crossing back and forth.

"She thinks she needs to say hello to everyone in sight," said Caitlin.

Upstairs along the hall a series of doors slammed in the draft, one after another.

"Guess-Who must be racing today," said Sophie.

Caitlin, studying the scene, nodded.

The crowd that showed up two hours later at the clubhouse was not large but it was dense. Everyone clustered together; they'd known each other a long time. Beneath the pyramid of yachting flags were familiar tennis hats and faded salmon shorts, warped topsiders and yellowing socks. Short, lime-green skirts, fashionable anywhere else in 1970, were here on North Eden nothing new. They were what the ladies wore and always had worn playing golf.

Apart from the crowd, slumped against the tackle shed, were the wayward teenagers in torn blue jeans and Indian prints. Caitlin and Sophie, among them, snuck drags from a furtive cigarette. Mum was sitting near the clubhouse doorway in front of a silver samovar, handing cups of tea upward with napkins pressed beneath. Chicky, the youngest Vincent, was waiting near her elbow for a cookie. According to their grandmother, Chicky looked exactly like Dad. She had said the same thing about each baby, as Mum had had them, seven of them one right after another. Caitlin and Sophie, the first babies, had been dressed in blue for the first years of their lives, in honor of the Blessed Virgin. Mum had been taught by nuns. After her seventh baby, she stopped listening to the pope. She was thirty-nine years old now, her last baby, Chicky, was six, and for the first time since marrying Dad, she had no little fists clutching at her hem, the way they would in department stores. "Hold on," she'd say before weaving off through crowded aisles.

"Just one," she whispered to Chicky. He snuck a

cookie from a china plate. Around the corner kids were lined up for ice cream being scooped out of a cardboard tub by freckled Amy Haffenreffer, who preferred the company of children. Out on the thorofare by the spindle, the last of the sailboats were tacking in to the finish line, each at a different angle, all at a heel.

Caitlin nudged Sophie. Mum was pouring a cup of tea. The man next to her had a grayish-white spot on the back of his dark head, and Mum's eyes were lit with a brightness. When her sister Grace visited, sitting on the porch in her smart wool dresses and silk kerchiefs and black sunglasses, telling New York stories, Mum would get that look, giggling now and then in an odd, excited way. The first time the girls had seen it had been years ago in the lamplight, when they'd all spent the night in the cabin on Boxed Island. Mum came flying out of the cricket darkness, her nightgown luminous, a fiery look in her eye. She was panting. On her way to the outhouse, she'd seen a fox, a silver fox. "It streaked across my path," she said. Her hands trembled and toyed with the ruffle at her neck; her pupils were lit in bright points from the oil lamp.

"No such thing," said Dad, thumping at a flimsy mattress.

Mum stood there transfixed. She turned to her babies, all six of them in diminishing sizes, rolled up in flannel sleeping bags. "As silver as the Silver Orient," she said. It was from a story they all knew, one Mum had read to them, about the train that took off from its tracks and flew over the Alps.

Later when the cabin was dark, Caitlin and Sophie heard Mum and Dad mumbling across the room. "Oh they'll forget about it by tomorrow," Mum said. But they didn't. It was one of those things they remembered and mentioned now and then, about that time the silver fox streaked across Mum's path and how her eyes were lit, not with fright, and how Dad said there was no such thing.

When Mum handed the man a cup of tea, the look was there: thrilled. Wilbur Kittredge had his collar turned up against his tanned skin. He was the head of a large international company. He made bombs.

The Kittredge estate was set high on a bluff of North Eden. The main house had a long porch that overlooked the bay where humped islands scattered off into tiny dots. The estate had stables and an electric fence and guest cottages and a walled-in garden where stone satyrs huddled, ears pointed, fingers secretly at their lips. They had exotic animals, antelopes and a snow leopard and crocodiles, and special guests. A Balinese fire dancer had performed under the moon; an American Indian had constructed an authentic teepee. The topiary garden was designed by an Italian monk to depict a tennis match. A man sculpted in privet served a green ball to a sculpted woman in a flared privet skirt crouched at a slender privet hedge. Each year the Kittredges had a clambake and invited the whole island—all the summer people, that is, and certain islanders who knew who they were. But the main attraction was the carriages. Wilbur Kittredge had over forty antique carriages lined up in a special barn. There were scenes painted on the shiny doors, polished brass railings, leather seats and velvet seats and fringed surreys with wicker sides. When Dad was home in Marshport during the week, Mum went on rides.

Wilbur Kittredge was a special friend of Mum's. Over the years, he'd sent her presents, strange items from strange lands. One package held an odd wreath of shellacked flowers, which Mum hung over the mitten basket. Caitlin and Sophie knew that if Dad had given her something like that it would have gone straight to the cellar. Some things just weren't Mum's taste. When his first son, Gus, was born, after three girls, Dad brought Mum gladiolas. To make it worse, they were yellow. His presents made Mum bite her lip; there was a whole world of things "not me" or "a little off." Dad learned to leave the sales slip in the box.

▼

The teenagers were discussing various figures in the crowd. "Ol' Will Kittredge is looking pretty dapper," said Westy Granger sullenly.

"Is your father up?" asked Trisha Holt, who had painted a rose on her cheek.

Everyone on the island minded each other's business. You always knew who was up or not. Everyone knew that Wilbur Kittredge's wife was at a spa in California.

"He got up yesterday," Sophie said. "He's probably at the garden." The vegetable garden was in the middle of the island on a bit of land their grandfather had bought long ago. The garden was one of Dad's projects. He'd grown the plants from seed in soil cubes that sat on a green plastic tray in the laundry room. He studied each seed as if it were a jewel, releasing it and brushing the dirt over with his baby finger. Each night he brought back something for supper: small clubs of zucchini, ripe tomatoes, string beans with their raw fiber-glass skin, and carrots luminous under creases of dirt.

Dad had other projects. For after-dinner, he liked to carve small birds. He was rebuilding the back walkway. There were mooring lines to be spliced onto buoys. When they were little, Dad built a lot of things, a bicycle hutch, a playhouse down in the woods, a treehouse with three separate platforms. Whenever a new baby came home, he'd built some-

65

thing for it. He constructed a bassinet with a step around it so the girls could stand and watch while Mum gave the baby a bath. They watched her fold the diapers fiercely, her eyes with an intent glare, clenching pins in her teeth, pins with plastic tulips on them.

To Caitlin and Sophie it seemed there always was a new baby. When it came home from the hospital, Caitlin and Sophie dressed up as Indians and made cards for Mum. The bundle got picked up and put down, and when it was left in its carriage, it lifted its head to stare at the back. Caitlin and Sophie looked into the black carriage at the baby's head bobbing around like a buoy, staring at nothing. It could stare at nothing for hours.

It was in the baby carriage that Frances died. She was the fifth baby. Only Caitlin and Sophie could remember it, being six and five. It was in the afternoon. Mum came home with shopping bags crinkling, wearing her Boston suit and with her hair in a puff from the hairdresser's. Delilah and Gus were there—everyone always came running into the hall when Mum came home. She picked Baby Frances out of the carriage where it was parked on the porch. Mum went tucking at the baby's throat. Suddenly she was in a hurry, pulling the baby tight to her, touching the baby's face. The kids all looked. Mum spat out, "Get down in the playroom," more mean than she'd ever yelled before. They weren't important anymore at all. Mum ran into the TV room and Caitlin saw her put her mouth on top of Baby Frances's mouth, trying to dial the phone at the same time. Then she slammed it down and went tearing out the hall and down the steps and onto the driveway toward the Birches'.

The next day and for a while after the driveway was filled with cars and the house with people. Caitlin and Sophie found ashtrays next to their toothbrushes in the bathroom and teacups on the piano bench. Baby Frances, they were told, was now in heaven and the grown-ups looked down at them as if they didn't understand. There were flowers everywhere, baskets on tables, pots on the floor, carefully shaped pyramids or clipped round globes.

One day, Sophie saw Mum sitting alone in the living room, where no one ever was, on the arm of a chair in a slouch. Her thumb moved slowly up and down her elbow, smoothing it over.

Downstairs in the playroom Caitlin said it was because Mum still missed Baby Frances. Sophie said she did too.

"Well," Delilah said, "I'm not going to die."

"You have to," Caitlin said. "Everyone in the world has to."

"Not me," Delilah said, pressing her eyelashes

down. "I'm going to be the first one in the world not to."

"But that's impossible, Delilah."

"Just wait."

They were all drawing pictures of the family, cards to give Mum and Dad. You lined everyone up according to age. In the sky they put an angel with a halo and wings and black hair for Baby Frances.

The next baby, Sherman, came less than a year after. He was a bad crier. He had a long high screech that would suddenly stop as if a switch had been thrown. After a long silence he'd launch again into even higher wails, gasps to make up for the time spent not breathing.

Among the tea drinkers on the wharf was a trio of strangers to North Eden, two swarthy men and a statuesque blond woman near the sail closet. They looked European.

"Kittredge houseguests," said Westy Granger.

"I bet they're folksingers," said Trisha Holt. "They look like Peter, Paul, and Mary."

"More like a Swedish movie star," said Westy's friend with the long hair. "Quite a T-shirt on her."

"The mystery woman perhaps," said Westy.

The other night they were careening home from a moonless party at Blind Man's Beach when they came upon a dark carriage clip-clopping along the Middle Road. Red lamps were swinging from points up front and there were two silhouettes under the fringed awning. The car slowed down and pulled to the side and everyone looked. Next to Mr. Kittredge was a woman with a hat on. Caitlin dug her elbow into Sophie's rib. A thin fly whip passed across the rosy lights, waving them on. Westy screeched forward and began to sing the chorus of an antiwar song and everyone joined in.

The fact that Mr. Kittredge made bombs did not, according to Mum, mean that he was bad. She recognized the bad guys. She threw her shoe at Nixon when he was on TV. She distributed leaflets after the bombing of Cambodia and gave cocktail parties with Patricia Meyer, the only other Democrat in Marshport, to raise money for their candidates. Years before, on a tour of the Capitol, they visited their senator and afterward Mum brought Caitlin and Sophie to visit Mr. Kittredge. Mum liked to look at other people's houses. While she was touring the greenhouse and the collection rooms and the new addition, Caitlin and Sophie swam in the Kittredges' slate pool without anyone watching, something they'd never done before. None of the other Kittredges were there but they never were. The afternoon air was hushed, with only heat bugs going, and when it started to rain, the girls slipped into the pool house. It had an automatic ice maker and ceramic elephants under glass tabletops, cushions trimmed in green bamboo patterns, and a pair of tusks taller than the girls, guarding the doorway. Silver frames showed the blond Kittredge daughters in bathing suits, waist-deep in turquoise water, glinting gold jewelry. When Mum and Mr. Kittredge got back, he lifted a trapdoor and led them down cement steps into a cement room, the bomb shelter. In the corner were boxes of dried food stacked up like bricks. Of all the things she saw, Mum said, the glass orchids were her favorite. Mum always told the girls her favorite things.

Wilbur Kittredge poked his head out of the clubhouse door and waved to the two men and the blond woman. They appeared amused with their surroundings, observing the scene with an air of irony. Wilbur Kittredge seemed to share their private joke and greeted them warmly when they joined him. Mum turned in her seat to be introduced, her shoulders stiff, her smile polite, and her eyes lightning-quick, taking it all in.

Before dinner each evening, Caitlin practiced her driving. She and Mum took the loop by the vegetable garden with the windows rolled down. Lumbering down the rutted road, the station wagon would scrape its fender on the deep holes, making Mum wince. This evening after the race tea when Caitlin looked over, Mum's face was pensive. A few strands of hair were caught in the side of her mouth but she didn't brush them away. They drove by the pond choked with lily pads and high-blown weeds, and passed the fence Dad had made. He'd also built a hitching post at the parking place and when they rounded the corner they found it occupied. Tied up to it was a horse and carriage.

"Oh," said Mum, sitting forward. The glint in her eye showed that she knew the carriage, and well. It was one of the smaller carriages, with a black hood curving over a double seat, no windows. The horse's long face was close to the car, its blinders out like absurd shutters, staring at them. Further back, in the gray shade of the bonnet, they could see the back of Wilbur Kittredge's head and the silvery spot on it. Behind him, with a different glow, was a white T-shirt arching upward.

"Turn around," Mum said.

Caitlin shifted into neutral and the engine roared.

"Back up." Mum was looking everywhere but forward. The car went stuttering backward in jerks. Once around the corner, they stopped and switched places and Mum drove home.

The wind dies down at that time of day and the bay past Clam Cove, its mud flat shiny, was pearly and still, a silk tablecloth with sailboats sitting on top, motionless.

"I didn't think we should get any nearer," said Mum after a while. "Those are especially spirited horses. They spook." The crease in her forehead hinted at deeper knowledge. Whatever it was, she kept it to herself.

Not long after, the island fell under the spell of a heat wave that wouldn't let up. It lasted for the rest of the summer. A limpid air hung over the glassy thorofare, which remained undulating and languid and pale blue. Screams and splashes could be heard day and night as kids ran drumming off the floats. Over the Labor Day weekend was the Kittredges' annual clambake, but the Vincents didn't go. Dad had played too long on the golf course that day and was out with heat stroke. He shut himself in his room, pulled the shades down, and lay in the dark. Mum, who sometimes went to parties without him, this year did not feel up to it and went to bed early too. At the end of the summer, the Vincents returned to Marshport and once again Wilbur Kittredge's post-cards appeared on the hall table—greetings from distant lands like Peru or Zanzibar or the Seychelle

Islands—cheerful notes dashed off in a loose, large hand, unsigned.

The following spring, after her fortieth birthday, Rosie Vincent gave birth for the eighth time. It was a girl, Miranda Rose. Everyone was excited; there hadn't been a baby in the house for years.

Mum sat up in bed in her pretty nightgown, the pillows behind her bordered in *fleurs-de-lis,* holding her new treasure. Everyone hovered around, knocking against the dust ruffle, lying diagonally at her feet. Mum gazed into the infant eyes, seeing their strange clarity. She touched the tiny nose. She uncurled the fiddlehead fists and showed them to everyone lolling around. "You see?" she said. "Her father's hands exactly."

Then came the feeding. They watched her unbutton the nightgown and feel inside for the bosom. After fixing it to the baby mouth, and satisfied with it, she looked up. Caitlin and Sophie saw it—that wild look—only this time there was something added. It was aimed at them and it said: There is nothing in the world compares with this.

The eye was fierce. The baby stayed fast. There is nothing so thrilling as this. Nothing.

PARTY BLUES

When their parents were away, the girls threw parties. They strung lights up around the driveway and dismantled the dining-room table to make room for dancing. They had the run of the place. People came from all over. The parties got huge.

It was April. Mum and Dad were in Bermuda with Chicky and Minnie, the two youngest Vincents. It wasn't late but the party was in full swing. Sophie could see the effects already—a rip in the canvas lawn chair, the begonia toppled over on the piano. Someone had been putting out joints in the Canton china. Sophie's boyfriend, Duer, had disappeared and she was on her second gin. She felt a bit off, despite the exuberance filling the house, despite the band's buoyant percussion. On her way upstairs, she passed someone carrying one of the good wine-glasses. The door to their parents' room was at the top of the hall. Sophie went to it. She closed the door behind her and was in the dark, quiet now with the rug. The chaise was a pale island; in the deeper darkness, still invisible, the huge bed.

The only time you came in here was for real emergencies. You knocked so softly they couldn't possibly hear. Only when the terror was enough would you finally dare to turn the knob and enter the big-bedded hush of their room. There would be the dim white shape of the covers and two dark heads, then Mum up on her elbow, the square neck of her night-gown showing, faint straps. "What is it, pumpkin?" she whispers and you hurry over, everything safe now, except you're in tears. . . .

As soon as Sophie's eyes got used to the dark, she took the ashtray off Dad's bedside table, pulled Mum's dressing-table bench to the window, and opened the sash. All the windows had sea views. She lit a cigarette.

At the lawn's edge she could make out ghostly forsythia, like rumpled fireworks. On top of everything else there was spring to bear. In the classrooms at college they went stir-crazy while the lilacs blew around in the hedges. Sophie could feel the bass

thumping in the soles of her feet. It would be a while
before anyone was dancing. They had to get high, if
not completely trashed. Sometimes you went to parties where no one danced at all. Even with the music
beneath her, she could hear the faint rush and thud
of the surf down on the rocks. The ocean had been
swimming today, astir beneath a spring mist, churn-
ing like a cauldron. She could see bits of light: across
the water were houselights on Andre's Point, stars
above, toward Boston the lighthouse on Stillman's
Island she'd watched flash all her life—first the white
blink then the red then the beam coming around and
the big white flash, meaning YOU. All she wanted
was for Duer to walk in the door.

It seemed to Sophie that it ought to feel different
to be alive. Her sisters came home for vacations,
threw big parties, remembered funny stories. Things
were a certain way and Caitlin and Delilah were that
way along with them. If she had been dropped down
in the jungle Sophie would have felt more at home.
They used to put on circuses next door with the
Birches. She'd liked that. There were home movies
of it. Caitlin in her ballerina costume with the span-
gles, Delilah as a tiger with whiskers drawn across
her cheeks. Sophie was a trapeze artist wearing a
cotton slip. She balanced the tightrope along the
brick garden wall, did a cartwheel. Coming right-side
up, bright-eyed and thrilled, she sees Mum's scowl-

ing face. "Your underpants were showing," Mum says under her breath.

. . . Or more at home in a decrepit café in the tough part of town . . . Across the sea . . . Instead she had found herself at the eggnog party at the Finches', dropped off for tennis cookouts at the Elysian Hunt Club, or pale and embarrassed at the Winter Cotillion. The way you had to conduct yourself in those outer rooms . . . it was like white death.

Duer wasn't about to walk in. He was more likely giving his undivided attention to a dazed fifteen-year-old developed beyond her years. Duer with his own lazy eyes, looking the girls up and down, rubbing his chest under his shirt. He had Sophie's heart, complete and entire. Duer was an eager blusher and when it came to the subject of love, he leaned into it. He slipped his hand under her shirt in the blossom tent of an elderberry tree and left it there, calmly cupped over her breast. They were talking about nothing, about this and that, and she thought so this is what love is. This was pure love when you had a boy's hand cupped over your breast, skin on skin and still you kept talking, a complete and utter understanding between you. She sat on his lap, feeling this complete and utter understanding. Which was the beginning of the problem, him having different ideas. Still, he was sweet with her; he paid her every attention. They found empty rooms and empty beds and empty spots under trees.

It had been love at first sight. Then, after hours in the French room with the lights on and the windows black, Duer first kissed her good-night and it stunned her and took her breath away. That had been four years ago.

The door burst open. People were always barging in on you. There was always someone going by the door slowly, eavesdropping, lingering in the hall. Two figures stood in the light, swaying. "Whoops," said Laura Leone, a tall figure at her side. Laura had a history of disasters, careless with herself, sloppy. "Out a here," she said in a low voice, then laughed at that and pushed the tall boy back into the hall. The door slammed.

Was that what two people were like when they were alone? When Sophie was little, they used to sneak out of bed and crouch at the top of the stairs, foreheads to the banister, and try to hear what Mum and Dad were saying down there in the TV room. Mostly they could only get the mumbles; sometimes they didn't hear a thing.

Sophie's parents had met on a double date at a football game. Mum had seen Gus Vincent before, though, dancing on a tabletop at the Silver Rim Ball on Beacon Hill. After they shook hands in the back-seat of a car, being introduced, Mum said she knew she would not marry him. His hands, she said, were not the hands she'd be married to for the rest of her life. They were perfectly fine hands, knuckling the back window in a little rhythm, but Mum said they weren't for her. She was wrong, of course. "Then how *did* you know?" Caitlin asks. Mum gets her enigmatic smile. "You just do," she says, her head shaking sympathetically; there are some things the girls simply can't know yet. Caitlin gets a faraway look, envisioning all the things in store.

When Mum announced to her friends she was marrying Gus Vincent, they warned her that life would be one long party. Mum loved parties. And for a while they did go to parties, despite all the babies. Mum would always drive home. On summer nights, she'd stop the car at Booth Cove and get out. The gate in the seawall was as wide as a barn door and creaked when she opened it. The water would be still and inky-black and very inviting and, in her pink evening gown, the satin one with rhinestones, she'd slip into the water, breaking the moon's reflection, taking a little dip. The splash of her kick drifted through the still air back to where Dad was sitting, nodding in the passenger seat. Nowadays Dad wouldn't go to a cocktail party if you paid him.

The door to her parents' room didn't catch after the slam and had swung open again. Sophie went to close it and paused with her hand on the knob and put her cheek to the door and pressed it there and rolled her face over the molding then jerked herself back.

She'd taken it hard—the discovery of her faults. Death was never far from her mind. One evening, Mum asked her to promise she wouldn't commit suicide until she was eighteen. "I think you'll outgrow it by then," she explained, casually doing her needlepoint in front of the TV.

But the dissatisfaction persisted. Sometimes it felt like a craving and when Duer was there she kissed and kissed, trying to kiss it away, to kiss herself into some calmness, or peace of mind.

She couldn't stay in this dark room all night, she'd better go back down. The hall was blazing. At the top of the stairs some girls were peering closely at the framed Christmas cards. "God, you guys must have had a blast growing up," said one, seeing Sophie. Sophie returned her smile weakly. Going down the stairs, Sophie met Delilah coming up.

"You seen Sherman?" Delilah asked.

Sophie hadn't. "I shudder to think," she said. Sherman, only twelve, already had a taste for pot.

They stood and watched with similar expressions of concern the clusters of people in the usually deserted hall. At the bar people pressed limes inside plastic glasses, making gin-and-tonics, pros at it. A bearlike fellow put out his cigarette on the floor. "Hoot Man!" someone cried. "What are you doing here, man?"

"Who are all these people?" Sophie said.

"Beats me," said Delilah. She leaned to whisper, "Did you see Frank came? Don't tell Caitlin."

Caitlin had had a brief fling with Frank; he'd gone up skiing with them. "Is this how good Catholic girls behave?" he asked with a bright leer. It didn't last long. He paid her too much attention, something that always gave Caitlin the creeps. After, he went around telling everyone, "Those girls do a number on you."

"She'd want to know, though," Sophie said.

Caitlin always went back to Eliot, whom she'd known the longest. Eliot was there for the weekend. Sophie asked Delilah if she'd seen Duer.

"No." Delilah shrugged. "Billy vanished hours ago, too." A smile flashed across her face. "Hey Andy!" she called down the stairs. "You're looking chipper tonight."

A boy in the crowd cast his deadpan eyes up at the sisters. "It's drug-induced," he said.

Sophie wandered into the living room, trying to affect hostess business. Delilah and Andy swept by, headed for the music in the dining room, handing her their glasses. Sophie sipped both drinks, put one down and kept the other. Giddy Meeks came hurrying over.

"Parker Harris is getting sick all over the down-stairs bathroom," she said. Giddy Meeks spent a lot of time with the Vincents.

"Great," said Sophie. "Don't tell Caitlin. She'll freak."

"Thanks," said Caitlin behind Sophie. "Why should I care? Let Delilah deal with it—he's her friend."

"Has anyone seen Duer?" Sophie asked.

"He was dancing with Mimi Vanden." Caitlin's voice lowered. "Frank's here," she said.

Giddy Meeks moved in closer.

"So I heard," Sophie said.

"He and Eliot have never met," Caitlin said with drama.

"Keep it that way," said Giddy Meeks.

Sophie headed in the opposite direction of the music. Mimi Vanden was one of those girls who sat with her back arched and held her neck taut like a ballerina. Her hair was a complete tangled mane and she raked her hands through it and tossed it over her shoulder. Mimi was as vague as a cloud. The boys drifted to her and leaned there, fascinated; she didn't seem to notice a thing.

Sophie turned back to Caitlin. "Is anyone sleeping in Mum and Dad's room?"

"I'm not," Caitlin said in a shocked voice. As if she'd never stayed in there. "I don't think anyone should."

"So do you want our room?"

"I was planning on it."

"Okay, Caitlin. I was just asking."

"Well, where else do you want us to sleep?"

"Fine, fine."

"Ask Gus," Caitlin said, changing to a helpful tone. "He'll let you stay in his."

Sophie went out on the terrace. People were sitting in the pink light, darker figures huddled around the keg.

"Are we on a hill?" asked a fellow gazing into the night.

A girl's voice said, "I think so. Why?"

"I just saw someone step off the edge."

Sophie spotted Duer walking up from the cars. They were parked in a wayward line all the way down the driveway and along the avenue.

"There you are," she said.

"Sophie-Dopher," said Duer, and came up to her and wrapped her in his arms, happy. He made them sway in a half-circle. He muttered things. "Okay," he said finally. "What's the matter?"

"Nothing," she said weakly. It was hard enough knowing what you thought without someone else's face an inch away.

"Come on, my gopher," he said and let his leg collapse, holding her hand up, meaning he was ready to dance.

They were dancing, with knees locked, when the

84

lights blew. The music spiraled into a deadening moan, then ceased altogether. "Is it a blackout?" someone cried. "This is perfect!" said a glad voice. Everyone was thrilled. Sophie heard Caitlin's voice: "We're *getting* the candles."

Sophie and Duer stood at the French windows and looked out. Andre's Point was completely dark, no lights at all. "It's all over," said Sophie.

"Soph," said Duer. "Relax."

"No," she said. "I mean, it's everywhere."

The candlelight quieted everyone down. You walked through rooms and could see the ends of people's legs, ankles crossed, then the rest of them in shadow, slumped in chairs, collapsed on sofas. An electric guitar was twanging out on the terrace, without its amplifier, sounding like an insect dirge.

When the lights came back on, there was a sigh of disappointment. Duer was gone again.

Sophie continued to wander about the house. Whenever you came home from school or after the summer, you'd wander through the house. They all did it, drifting from room to room alone, reacquainting themselves with familiar things. You touched the stone madonna, picked up the butterfly paper-

weight. In the silver cigarette box you'd find a marble
or a button. You tried the jade lighter with its lighter-
fluid smell, never expecting it to work and it never
did. But there was always a feeling of possibility.
Things might be different. You might find something
you'd forgotten about. You opened drawers: there
was the brass hook with the eagle wings, the circular
matchboxes covered with marbleized paper, a pack
of cards in a blue and white case.

Sometimes you did find unexpected things. That
fall when Sophie had her wisdom teeth out, she'd go
on wanders like that in her nightgown, drug-dazed
through the empty house, looking at the stuff on
people's bureaus. One afternoon, heading for Delilah's room and the view, she stopped in the doorway, surprised to find Mum in there taking a nap.
She was lying on her side, facing the wall, and her
shoulders were shaking up and down, crying. Sophie
turned away quietly, her heart loud inside.

They were all a bunch of snoops, the whole family.
Growing up, if you wanted to save anything you had
better hide it. Sophie had cubbyholes in her desk,
good for barricading. The bags of candy would never
last left out in the open.

There was some hooting out on the driveway—die-
hards heading for the beach. Cars revved, doors

were slamming, horns honked. They hardly needed their headlights; the sky had lifted into a deep royal blue. Delilah was standing up in the back of Billy's yellow pickup, screaming directions. She kicked a leg out of the slit in her skirt like a showgirl. "Let's cruise!" she cried and banged on the yellow hood. "Surf's up!"

Sophie carried glasses into the kitchen. She collected cups and set them down in little groups on tables. She kept looking around. People's advice was: You don't find it when you're looking. Therefore, you had to pretend not to be looking. Then something would come drifting along like down a river. But surely not everyone would be fooled—God, for one.

The Catholics said that God was always watching, everything you did. He even knew what went on in your mind. Even when she said she didn't believe in God, it was hard to get rid of the feeling that someone somewhere was watching.

Once the air lightened into pale blue, Sophie felt she could go to bed. It was like sleepwalking doing anything at that hour—all the cigarettes, all the drinks. The lawn lay under a light mist and plastic cups were scattered about on their sides. For weeks to come there would be stories—who walked in on whom, flat tires on the way home, how disheveled Laura Leone looked, stumbling out of the woods at four A.M.

Sophie listened at the bedroom door before opening it very slowly. She and Caitlin had shared a room throughout elementary school. There were faded tissue-paper flowers on the lampshades—Caitlin's decoration; a peace sign still dangled from a pink wool ribbon. In Caitlin's bed were sacked out two big lumps. Sophie untied her dress, took off her earrings, wrapped herself in an Indian shawl.

Caitlin opened one eye and whispered, "Are people still here?"

"Sort of."

The eye shut with exhaustion. "Okay," she said. "Night," already drifting into sleep.

Sophie slipped into the hall. She pulled a puff out of the linen closet and dragged it, unraveling, down the narrow corridor. This was where they used to play while their bath was running, their turtlenecks in floppy turbans on their heads, tearing down to the dark end and pivoting FAST before the goblins came winging out, latching on to your chest, sucking the breath out of you. The goblins lived in the back of the house. On rainy afternoons, with the lights on, they'd go into the mattress room and jump around and press up against one another.

In the last room at the end of the corridor Sophie

found Duer. The mournful wail of a saxophone could be heard in the thin air. Out the window she saw Charlie Asher strolling off down the driveway in a rumpled white suit, playing his horn.

"Good ol' Chuck," said Duer underneath a pillow.

Sophie got in and the bed was warm; Duer was always warm. They had a sweet warm time. No bed was too small for Duer and Sophie. After he passed out, she stared at his face, marveling at the mouth. She touched the outline. His lips kissed her finger but the rest of him was halfway to dreamland.

She lay herself alongside him, adjusting herself, fitting. Through the door the first sun hit the wall. The orange light was reflected off some pictures, ricocheting into corners. It was something, the way it looked. It pained her. She should be glad—in a boy's arms, no fatal disease, a house filled with friends—but something was still wrong.

Mum used to read them a story—Sophie had noticed it in Minnie's room when she was showing someone where to sleep—about the schoolchildren lining up for outings in Paris. In the middle of the night, Miss Clavell wakes up. "Something is not right!" she says. That was the feeling. Miss Clavell checks the long row of beds with a flashlight and when she gets to the last bed, finds it empty. One of the little girls is gone.

THE NAVIGATOR

In the summer they ate early, everyone drifting home like particles in a tide. By evening most of the people had disappeared from the wharf and the North Eden harbor was quiet, the thorofare running by as flat as a slab of granite. Tonight there was a fog coming in. It was the end of August and all seven of the Vincent children were up there in Maine.

Gus came in off the dock. The screen door ticked out its long yawn, and when he reached the kitchen at the end of the short hall it clapped shut.

The girls were making dinner. Delilah shook salt into the pots on the stove; Sophie peeled a cucumber.

Gus propped his foot against the icebox and bumped against the doorframe.

"Work hard?" Sophie said.

Gus nodded. He had been house painting all summer; his dark skin was specked with white.

Sophie ran a fork down the side of the cucumber while she held it up next to Gus's face. "For your skin," she said. He closed his eyes to feel the spray.

Delilah folded her arms. "It's just us tonight," she said. "Mum and Dad are going to the Irvings'."

"Dad is?" Gus said. "What is it, skit night?"

"Practically," Sophie said. She picked up a cigarette from the ashtray, took a drag, and gave it to Gus. "They're playing find-the-button."

Gus smiled. "Which one's that?"

"You know. They hide the things—a thimble on the lampshade or a golf tee in the peanuts—the button camouflaged in some flowers. When you spot it, you write it down."

"How'd Mum get him to go?" Gus rubbed the ash into his pants. The bottoms were rolled up in doughnuts.

"God knows," said Sophie.

"It was a choice between that and the Kittredges' clambake on Sunday," Delilah said.

They all laughed.

Delilah was crumbling hamburger. "Poor guy," she said to the frying pan.

92

"He can handle it," Sophie said.

Gus left them and went into the living room. Chicky, the youngest of the boys, was sitting on the creaking wicker sofa. Going by, Gus swatted the back of his head. On the record player, Bob Dylan was singing "Tangled Up in Blue" for the millionth time. Certain records stayed in North Eden all year long—they were the rejects, hopelessly warped. Still, they got put on again and again. Hearing those songs straight through somewhere else was always a surprise.

Gus took his book off the pile of *National Geographic* and *Harvard* magazines. He stretched out on the window seat, opened the book, and set it facedown on his stomach.

"Went to the quarry," Chicky said. He was whittling at a stick with his Swiss Army knife. "The bottomless one."

"Right," Gus said. He smiled out the window at the floats. The Jewel girls were down there climbing out of their stinkpot. A light mist drifted by in thin trails.

"It was," Chicky said. Shavings littered the floor by his bare feet.

"Chicky, it's impossible," his older brother said. "Quarries're man-made."

Chicky worked over a little knot. "You can think what you want," he said.

From the kitchen, Sophie called, "Where's Minna?" The boys didn't answer. The screen door slammed. "I'm right here," came the six-year-old voice from the hall. Sophie and little Miranda came into the living room at the same time from separate doors.

Sophie said, "Will someone go tell Ma?"

"Is it supper?" Gus asked.

"Five minutes."

"Good," Chicky said.

"Who's going to tell Ma?" Sophie said, holding a stack of napkins at her throat.

Minnie climbed onto Gus's lap and perched on her shins. Gus said, "Minnie will, won't she, Minniana?"

"Do I have to?"

"I would but we're getting supper," Sophie said. She stepped into the dining room but stayed within earshot.

"I always do," said Minnie, collapsing on her brother.

Caitlin walked in. "You always do what?" she asked. Her hair was wet and she hit at it from underneath to dry.

"Well, somebody better go," Sophie said from the dining room. Her head appeared. "Gus, will you?"

Gus winced.

"What?" Caitlin said.

"Why don't you ask Sherman?" Chicky said. He pointed out the window. "He never goes."

Sherman, the middle brother, was standing outside at the dock railing. He was spitting over the edge and watching it land in the water. Someone must have tapped on the window above him—Mum and Dad were upstairs getting dressed—because Sherman turned and looked up. His eyes revealed nothing, like Indian eyes.

"Sure," Sophie said. "Good luck."

Minnie kept her head against Gus's chest. *"He's* not about to get Ma," she said.

"Why not?" Caitlin said. She huffed over to the window and lifted it. A damp mist came rolling over the sill. "Sherman," she said, her voice sounding cottony outside. "Go tell Ma it's supper."

Sherman turned his head. "Why don't you?" he said.

"Because I'm asking you to."

Sherman glanced past her. "Why doesn't Chicky go?" he said.

"I don't believe this," Sophie said.

Chicky's knife peeled a long curl. "She'll come over anyway," he said.

Caitlin turned around to him with her mouth set.

Delilah stood in the doorway with a potholder mitten on. "Has someone gone to get Ma?"

95

"Gee, Delilah," Gus said. "We thought you'd gone."

"This is ridiculous," Caitlin said. "Come on, Minnie. Go."

Minnie's little back went stiff. "I always do." She shifted off Gus.

"It's not going to kill you," Caitlin said.

Minnie trudged out of the room. They heard the screen door swing, then slam. From where he sat, Gus could see her padding over on the dock to Ma's house. He made a moping face and rocked from side to side, imitating her.

The girls laughed.

The dining room had cream-colored walls and two windows that faced the harbor. At high tide, the water rose right up to the shingles and the light made crisscrossing patterns on the low ceiling. It was a small room, just fitting the long table.

Ma, Dad's mother, lived by herself in the far house. Her cook, Livia, had gone back to Ireland, so then kitchen was no longer used. Before supper, Ma read in her living room and had glasses of sherry. By the time she got to the other house for dinner with her grandchildren, her face was flushed.

She sat down, wobbling, at her usual place.

Delilah had a plate at the side table. "Sherman, can you wait? I'm getting this for Ma."

Ma had on a smile. She smiled at the children, smiled at the candle flame, smiled at the blue bowl of grated cheese. "Isn't this nice," she said, smiling. Four small vases of nasturtiums from the garden were on the table.

Gus stood at the window, holding his plate over his chest. "Foggy," he said.

"Is it?" Sophie said. She was busy with wooden spoons in the salad. Everyone bustled around. Caitlin poured milk for Minnie.

Gus nodded and touched his forehead to the pane. "Everything's disappearing," he said.

They'd been eating for a while when Dad came in. He rubbed his hands together. "Evening, evening," he said, shifting from one foot to the other.

"You look pretty snappy," Sophie said. He was wearing a yellow blazer and a tie with green anchors on it. His face looked freshly slapped.

"Mum assures me I won't be allowed in Lally Irving's house without the proper attire," he said, bent slightly at the waist.

"You look great," Caitlin said.

Dad smiled dismissively.

Mum came in smelling of perfume, wearing a long skirt. "See you later, monkeys," she said. She plucked a carrot stick from the salad.

Ma beamed at Mum. "Rosie," she said.

Mum's real name was Rose Marie—it was Irish—but she'd changed it, thanks to Dad. He called her

Rosie after the schoolteacher in *The African Queen* who dumps out all of Humphrey Bogart's gin in order to get them down the river. Mum never drank at all.

She looked at her family in the candlelight. "Okey-dokey," she said.

"Good luck finding the button," Gus said.

"Who needs luck?" Mum said, kicking out her foot. "You're looking at last year's champ. Come on, Uncs, off we go."

Dad bowed, putting his palms together, and followed after her. Everyone at the table chuckled. Ma was smiling. She held her fork over her plate but still had not touched her food.

Early the next morning Gus woke up the boys to explain what had happened.

"They got home from the Irvings'," Gus said, "and Mum couldn't get him down the steps."

There were five flights of granite that led down from the street. Gus and the girls had heard Mum call "Yoo hoo." Gus went up the steps to help Dad down. The girls stood in the floodlight of the underpass, watching in the fog. Gus and Mum brought him into the light. Collapsed between them, Dad had been smiling grandly. He caught sight of his daughters in a semicircle and beamed toward them. Receiving no response, he had made a *whoops* expression and covered his mouth, giggling.

Gus sat on Sherman's bed but faced Chicky. "We're going to talk to him this morning," he said.

"What for?" Sherman said. "Let the guy do what he wants."

The girls were downstairs with Mum, except for Minnie, who was at sailing class.

"He didn't want to go in the first place," Mum said, washing dishes at the sink. "I shouldn't have made him."

Caitlin waited by the toaster. "What happened?" she asked.

"He was okay till dinner," Mum said. She gazed through the window in front of her; the shingles of the house next door were a foot away. "Then halfway through the roast beef he decided he was finished and plopped his plate down on top of Mrs. Aberdeen's."

They all smiled in spite of themselves.

"What did Mrs. Aberdeen do?" Delilah said.

Mum shook her head.

Caitlin was serious. "Then what?"

"He collapsed on his place mat with his hands over his head." Mum turned to her daughters. "He said, 'This is so *boring.*'"

Caitlin was still. "You're kidding."

"Then—" Mum took a breath. "Everyone pretended it was time to go and they put their jackets back on and we all said good-bye and they helped Dad find his way to the car. After we drove off, I imagine they went back in and finished dinner."

Sophie said, "You mean they faked going home?"

Mum shrugged: that was nothing.

The boys were shuffling in. Mum said, "He won't listen to me. I'm like a buzz in his ear."

They waited at the table, the girls at the near end, the boys next to the windows.

Sophie heard Dad and set down her knife. Delilah straightened her spine. Dad came in with his plate and put it down. Caitlin bit delicately into her muffin, stealing glances in Dad's direction. Dad went back into the kitchen and returned with a carton of orange juice. He poured a glass and drank it standing up.

Mum was beside him, holding the back of her chair. Her scarf was rolled into a hair band above her wide forehead. She had on a lavender turtleneck.

"The kids want to talk to you, Uncs," she said and slipped into her seat.

Dad pulled out his chair noisily. He buttered his toast, not waiting for the butter to melt. "You ready for a little golf today, Sherman?" he said, not looking up.

Gus looked at Sherman, then at his father, then at Mum. Mum was pressing crumbs with her fingers and brushing them off, making a little pile. Chicky was interested in something under the table. He made a noise to call the cat. Sherman sat heavily, no breakfast plate in front of him, his hands in his lap.

Caitlin spoke first. "Do you remember last night?"

Dad's chin traced out a long nod.

"How's your arm?" Delilah asked.

"My hand," he said and held it up. "Stiff." He put it back down and with his good hand folded some toast around his bacon and took a bite.

Halfway down the steps, he had broken free of Gus and Mum and keeled over into the unguarded rubble. There had been a trickling of small stones after him. The girls watched helplessly as he got onto his hands and knees. His head had wobbled like one of those toy dogs people have on their dashboards. The girls looked away.

"Dad, do you remember talking to me?" Gus said.

"Yes," said his father, addressing the jar of beach-plum jelly before him.

"What?" Delilah said.

Dad's frown was like a twitch. "Yes," he repeated.

"Do you remember what you said you'd do?" Gus asked.

Dad dipped his rolled-up toast into his mug of coffee. He nodded.

"Well?" Caitlin said. "What about it?"

Dad chewed, keeping his mouth closed. He looked around the table with an innocent expression.

Sophie said, "We have to talk about it."

"Fine," he said.

While Gus was bringing him upstairs, the girls had lingered in the hall with Mum. Above them, they heard Gus's urgent voice. They sat on the bottom step, transfixed. His voice was pleading, "We all do . . . because whenever we try . . . can't stand it when you . . ."

Outside some footsteps had banged by—two figures in yellow slickers passed the doorway—their steps ringing woodenly on the dock. But the girls hardly noticed, glancing over like sleepwalkers. The fog blew by through the underpass.

Above them they had heard Dad say, "Imagine that."

Caitlin covered her knuckles and slouched forward on the table. "So will you stop?" She looked at Mum. Mum was gazing out the window.

Dad looked at Caitlin as if she were speaking another language.

Sophie said, "You have to, Dad," and her voice wavered. Dad turned to her with the same face, blank but suspecting insult.

"Well?" Caitlin said.

Chicky pointed toward the water. "Look," he said.

Everyone turned. A huge green cattle boat had entered the window frame, undulating behind the tiny streaks in the glass. The white sails were as flat as building sides. It changed the light in the dining room.

"Looks like the *Horn of Plenty,*" Mum said brightly.

Everyone watched it glide into the second window.

"No," Sherman said. It was a mystery how he knew these things. "That's *Captain's Folly.*"

When Dad was young he had worked summers on a cattle boat that cruised through the islands. He'd been the navigator. He still had an astronomy book on the bottom shelf of his bedside table.

"Is it anchoring?" Sophie said.

Delilah shook her head. "It's just passing through."

The sailboat slipped out of the window frame. Gus tipped back his chair to keep it in sight. It continued through the thorofare. At the outer cove, its sails buckled and a tiny figure at the bow lowered a huge anchor into the water. Gus set his chair down and faced back in.

Dad hit the table with his hand like a gavel and started to get up.

"Wait," Caitlin said. "Dad." His frown was attentive. She ducked and went on, "We think you need help."

Dad glanced at Mum. She was fiddling with her pearl earring. Her other hand came up for an adjustment.

"You do, Dad," Sophie said.

Dad's gaze went over the table—the green vases of red nasturtiums, some Sugar Pops casting pebble shadows. . . . He reached into his pocket, hitching up his whole side as if mounting a horse. "Okay," he said uncertainly. He brought out a pack of cigarettes and stirred his finger in the opening. When he lit one, it burned halfway down in the first drag.

Sophie covered her forehead. "Okay what?" she said.

Dad looked at her with a cold eye. Delilah nudged her; she kept facing Dad. His posture was stiff and erect and his lips were pressed smartly together.

Caitlin lifted her chin toward him. "Okay what?" she said.

His eyes glared. She shrank back. As he put out his cigarette, his throat seemed to swell, as if his Adam's apple were expanding and the whole of his uncomfortable being were struggling there in his throat. He coughed. "I won't drink," he said.

Was that it? Caitlin began to smile. Sophie picked up a muffin crust and tapped it on her plate.

Gus said, "But, Dad, do you think—?"

"I said, 'I won't drink.' "

"I know, but . . ." Gus inspected his hands lying flat in front of him.

Delilah said, "That's great, Dad."

Dad's chair scraped the floor and he stood up. Mum had a satisfied face. "Okay, monkeys," she said, "where shall we take the picnic?"

104

▼

The sky was smooth, blue and clear. Ma watched from her balcony while they streamed out to the boat. A book lay in her lap. She had stopped going on picnics. Each one said good-bye to her, passing beneath her with their towels and books and baskets. Ma held a cigarette pinched elegantly between thumb and finger. The skirt of her print dress stirred against the chair.

Random River was at the end of one of the coves that scalloped off the thorofare. A tidal river, it was a muddy bed dotted with boulders at low tide. When the tide was high, a boat could motor up there. Even then, rocks appeared, just breaking the surface.

Dad stood at the wheel of the fiber-glass motorboat. His seven children were arranged in various perches; the motor gurgled at a slow speed. Mum sat beside him behind the windshield with her round sunglasses on. Usually there was much advice about the rocks, or Dad would appoint a lookout. "You're heading right for one!" "No no! To the left!" Today, there wasn't a peep. Dad navigated his way down the swirling turns, over the dimpled water.

It was glassy along the shore, the water dark green and shaded, bugs leaving pinpricks here and there. Bristling out of the rocks was the stiff grass—a porous leaf that slashed your calves when you were wading. There were tiny slugs clinging to the blades.

The Vincents glided toward their rock. They always went to the same rock. It had a plateau where the picnic basket got put and a scooped-out place where you could lie in the sun. In the photo albums there were lots of pictures taken here.

Gus stepped over the bow railing and crouched at the front.

"Careful," Mum said.

He leapt onto the rock and turned to fend off the bow.

"Eggshell landing," Caitlin said.

They all felt the crunch. "Whoops," Sophie said. But nothing was going to disturb the dreamy contentment that had taken over.

They unloaded, balancing cushions and coolers, lowering Minnie by her armpits. Delilah gripped Mum's arm while she stepped down. At the stern, Dad flung the anchor into the water. Gus led the painter into a jumble of rocks.

The sun streaked across the long ripples of the lagoon. Had Ma been there, she'd have already been in. Sophie tested the water. Everyone moved about politely. Caitlin squinted into the sun, then laid out her towel. She tugged the towel over to make room for Sophie. Mum pulled Minnie's sweatshirt over her head and her pigtails popped out.

"Listen to this," Delilah said. She had a magazine

across her thighs. " 'The two hundred couples exchanged vows beneath a grape bower on the Reverend's California estate.' "

"Sick," Mum said. She settled her head back on Minnie's life jacket.

" 'Afterwards, the wedded devotees reaffirmed their faith in a baptismal ceremony in the garden fountains.' "

"Unbelievable," Caitlin said.

Sherman was rummaging around in the picnic basket. He stood up with a handful of Fritos and crunched them one at a time. Dad carried the cooler up higher into the shade. There was a toppled tree up there, with roots that spread in a fan. When they were younger, the kids used to stand in front of it and hoot and listen for the echo. It was like a half-shell, the way the sounds reverberated. Up close, the roots and moss made intricate designs, like an ancient chart. Chicky was digging at a groove in the rock with a stick, idly but persistently. Gus and Minnie squatted over some curly black lichen. "Indian cornflakes," Gus said. Minnie laughed. It was quiet and pleasant and there was no noise except the drone of a motorboat somewhere out on the water.

Then they all heard the sound.

They sometimes heard noises far off—a *crack* like that—someone with a shotgun who knew what he was doing, or a pickup backfiring on the South Eden

bridge farther down the river. But none of the pic-
nickers mistook this sound.

Some heads jerked toward Dad; some looked
down. Above them, Dad was facing the root screen,
his back to the family. Mum didn't move, lying on the
life jacket, eyes hidden behind her sunglasses. Sophie hugged her shins and bit her knee. Gus's neck
was twisted into a tortured position; he glared at
Dad's back.

Dad turned around. He gazed with an innocent
expression out over the snaking water. If aware of
the eyes upon him, Dad did not betray it, observing
the scenery with contentment; nothing more normal
than for him to be standing in the shade at a family
picnic holding a can of beer. He twisted the ring from
its opening and, squinting at a far-off view, stooped
to lap up the nipple of foam at the top of the can.

The silence was no longer tranquil.

Sometimes on still, black nights they had had
throwing contests off the dock. They threw stones
into the thorofare and listened to hear them land.
Sometimes the darkness would swallow up a stone
and they'd wait, but no sound would come. It
seemed then as if the stone had gone into some
further darkness, entered some other dimension
where things went on falling and falling.

ACCIDENT

Caitlin and Delilah are blabbing away in the kitchen. Sherman, who's in the TV room next to a screen window, can hear them, down at the end of the porch, where they've got the back door open. The girls never stop talking, worrying about their boy-friends, worrying about Dad, always having fits—especially since their mother died. Sherman behaves like his father and ignores them. Mr. Vincent is in there with him, sitting on the other couch in the dim light, with his book and his drink. They both watch when the sports comes on. Sherman has the cat in his lap, not thinking much, sixteen years old.

The smell from the kitchen fills the whole downstairs. "We're having roast beef," says Sherman, looking at the cat's paw and pressing it so the claws come out. Mr. Vincent turns his face and registers this information with a nod. Then he goes back to his book.

The girls take turns running the house. Of the seven kids in the family, only five are at home now. Gus, who's nineteen, is in Kennebunkport for the summer, mapping and injecting trees for a forestry service. Sophie, who comes between Caitlin and Delilah, took off for Colorado with some friends when Delilah moved home. Sophie had been there since the winter, when their mother was killed. Caitlin, who is twenty-three, lives in Cambridge and works for a woman who collects art. She comes out to Marshport on the weekends to go to the beach and also, she says, to be with Dad.

The girls yell for Sherman to come set the table. If his younger brother were there, Sherman would make him do it, but Chicky is out at his friend Richard's house. Sherman drops the cat on the rug and traipses down the hall, past all the coat hooks and into the bright-yellow kitchen.

"Set it for seven," says Delilah. She's the dark one, the smallest, with a chunky waist but the rest of her like bird bones. "Hal's coming out after work." She used to live in Somerville with Hal, who's a carpenter. They met in college. When Hal comes out for the weekends, he slips off to Sherman and Chicky's room and smokes pot with them. Delilah usually gets high, too—only later, after Mr. Vincent has gone to bed and they bring the bong into the TV room.

Sherman takes down some plates.

"Not those," says Caitlin. She's flipping the roast potatoes in the oven but looks over her shoulder to see what he's doing. "Use the Harvard plates."

He puts the blue and white plates around the table that they've been eating at all their lives—white with a yellow trim. Underneath are metal things that jab into your knees. When they were young, they came down for breakfast and their mother would have set it the night before—six bowls, one at each place. Only six, because Minnie wasn't born yet—she came later.

"Yah," says Delilah, supervising. "Those are good." Mr. Vincent doesn't like to eat in the big dining room, so they squeeze in here. With everyone sitting, you can barely get between the counter and the table.

Then the girls start in. First Delilah says, "Have you thought about what you're going to do this summer?"

Sherman opens a drawer. "Get a job," he says.

"Do you have any idea what?" Caitlin leans against the icebox, arms folded, waiting.

"Nope." He puts the forks on the left, the knives on the right.

Delilah lights a cigarette from a burner. "Have you even started looking?" she asks.

"Not yet."

"Chicky has a job with Mr. Lewis," says Caitlin.

"Yup," Sherman says. Mr. Lewis's son, Richard, happens to be Chicky's best friend.

"Dad's not going to let you stay at home if you don't have a job."

"I know." His sisters watch while he folds the napkins into triangles.

"So what are you going to do?" Caitlin asks.

"Get a job," he says, to shut her up.

"Sherman," she says. Her forehead wrinkles. "What do you expect? That a job's going to come find you?"

He turns a plate so the building on it is right-side up.

"Leave him alone, Caity," says Delilah, and puts her cigarette out under the faucet. "He'll get a job. Won't you, Sherman?"

"Hope so." He steps back from the table, finished.

"Thanks," says Delilah. "Is Chicky back yet?"

"Dunno." He turns to walk out.

"Wait," she says. "Are you going to that party tonight?"

"What party?" asks Caitlin, lightening up.

Delilah makes it sound like a big deal. "Chicky's

friends are having a party at Richard's by Jingle Beach."

"Fun," says Caitlin encouragingly. The girls have parties at the house—huge ones. Some kids from town crashed the last one and refused to leave. Mr. Vincent was next door at the Drapers', spending the night, away from the blaring music. Gus picked a fight and made a dent in the plaster. Caitlin called the cops.

"You should go," Delilah tells Sherman. "Why not?"

Sherman retreats to his room to get a quick buzz before dinner. He and Chicky share the maid's room downstairs, at the back of the house. It's where they spend most of their time, away from everybody, playing Bob Marley nonstop. On the walls are some of Sherman's drawings—abstract ones that look like shattered panes of glass. One charcoal sketch, on Chicky's side of the room, is of Mum. The smile looks flat, because Sherman did it from a photograph. She has her sunglasses on and is wearing pigtails.

Sherman sips his joint in front of the window. The kitchen bell rings, calling Minnie home. Then Sherman hears, down at the marsh, the familiar rattle of the train going by, the train that hit Mum's car and killed her. Sherman has certain theories about the accident, and about the family, and gives them to

113

Chicky late at night, each in his bed—brothers. Sherman can tell his brother things he knows won't get repeated, especially to the girls.

The other night, with the reggae going, Sherman said, "As soon as I get enough money, I'm going to the West Indies. To live."

"You are?" said Chicky. Sherman always had these schemes.

"Yup," said Sherman, wide awake.

There was silence on the other side of the room, and Sherman could practically hear his brother thinking. Finally, Chicky said, "Okay. I'll meet you there."

Out the window Sherman sees Minnie at the end of the driveway, pushing her bike up the hill. She gets back on and rides fast, her seven-year-old legs pedaling furiously, her pigtails out like stiff brushes. She abandons her bike on the slope of the lawn, then runs around to the porch. Sherman smirks, feeling the pot. From listening all his life, he can tell that a car down on the avenue is turning up their driveway, and, sure enough, Hal's heap turns toward the house, rumbling and ticking, about to stall.

Delilah calls, "Hello, honey," from the porch. Hal gets out, grabbing cigarettes off the dashboard. Minnie's voice goes, "Hi, Hal," and then Sherman sees her hanging over the porch railing. Delilah says, "You have time for a quick shower," and Sherman snickers, hearing that.

114

When the bell rings again, it means it's supper-time. Going into the kitchen, Sherman answers the phone.

"That better be Chicky," says Delilah, making gravy at the stove. "Where is he? Tell him we're eating this second."

Keeping the receiver close, Sherman turns away. Chicky's still at Richard's, staying for dinner. "Wanna come to this party later?" he asks Sherman. "Then you can give me a ride home." Chicky is at the age when his voice sounds like water gurgling—first loud, then soft and far away.

"All right," Sherman says. They'll probably have pot. Chicky's friend Bruce usually has good pot.

Delilah is still blabbing away. "Typical Chicky. Where is he? Why didn't he call before?"

Sherman hangs up.

"Well?" Caitlin asks.

"He's staying there for supper."

"Thanks a lot for telling us," says Delilah. Minnie is already at her place, the table up to her neck.

Mr. Vincent strides in, patting his chest pockets. "Another culinary delight? What have we here?" He pushes in some chairs and peers into the bowls on the counter.

"Chicky just called," Delilah tells him. "He's eating at Richard's." She waits for his reaction.

"Splendid, splendid," says Mr. Vincent. He parks himself by the sink and waits to go last, his wrists

115

tucked under his armpits. Caitlin starts Minnie's plate, and Sherman goes next. "Don't take so many onions," she says, and he drops a couple back with his fingers. Chicky always gets out of it—being at home.

Hal comes in with his hair slicked back after his shower. He's wearing a purple shirt that Delilah gave him. "Hello, Mr. Vincent," he says, before doing anything. Delilah waves his plate for him to take.

"Good evening to you, Hal." Mr. Vincent keeps his heels tightly together.

"Come on, Dad," says Caitlin. "Come get some food."

He nods at her back; he'll go when he's ready. Delilah puts Chicky's milk at Hal's place and removes the extra setting.

The last one to sit down is Mr. Vincent, at the head. Delilah says, "I got a letter from Gus." She looks down at her father's plate. "Is that all you're having? Aren't you taking any broccoli?"

He says, "We'll have broccoli from my garden in late July. Please pass the gravy, Minnie my love."

Minnie doesn't move, so Sherman pokes her.

"What did Gus say?" Caitlin always puts huge chunks of butter on her potatoes.

"He and Bub are living in a tent."

Mr. Vincent rolls his eyes. "Good ol' Gus," he says wearily.

116

"He is?" asks Minnie. She holds on to her fork with a tiny fist. "Where?"

"In the woods," says Delilah, talking with her mouth full. "They have Dinty Moore every night."

"Yuck," says Caitlin.

"What's dinty more?" asks Minnie.

Delilah points her knife in the air, like a teacher. "From a can."

Sherman feels a paw bat his calf, and slips a piece of meat to the cat under the table. His father notices this and frowns, but doesn't say anything.

"And they hear bears roaming around at night," Delilah says.

"Really?" Minnie believes everything.

"You'll be pleased to know the lettuce is coming along superbly," says Mr. Vincent. "We should have some next week."

"Good," says Caitlin. Everyone eats.

The back door is open behind Mr. Vincent, and with no one talking they can hear clearly the train rattling by down through the woods, along the marsh. Then it clatters off faintly. Sherman glances at Hal and can tell by his slow chewing that the noise makes him nervous. Everyone else keeps on with the meal, ignoring it, acting as if they're used to it by now.

▼

117

When they left the party, Sherman walked smack into a privet hedge on his way to the car. Chicky stopped on the gravel, his long arms hanging down. "I don't think you better drive," he said.

"Well, I am," said Sherman. He cast a glance back at his brother, his face almost cross-eyed from drinking. "Come if you want."

Chicky watched him get in the little Volkswagen. Inside at Richard's, music was playing, and a softened bass thumped in the night. Chicky thought for a moment, but he didn't know how else to get home.

Sherman drove fast down the side streets, under the leafy shadows of the streetlights. When they came into town, which was lit up and empty, he accelerated to fifty. Chicky kept quiet in his seat. At the fork, the car headed straight for the Wayward Dog Tavern.

"Sherman!" Chicky grabbed the wheel to make the corner.

Sherman jerked his elbow up and knocked his hand away. "Cut it out," he said. He was flooring it.

Chicky braced himself on the dashboard and thought, This is it, we're going to die, whipping past the houses at one o'clock in the morning. They saw no other cars, luckily, since Sherman was straddling the line the whole time. On the straightaway, Chicky sat back slightly. Then, at the Lighthouse Inn, the car made the turn at a tilt, just missing the center island.

They bounded over the roller-coaster hills on Sea Street, and turned onto Chatham Avenue, nearly sideswiping a stone pillar.

Then Chicky said, "Let me out." They had come to the top of the hill before the road curved around the beach. Sherman jammed on the brakes. "You're too drunk," Chicky pleaded, on the verge of tears. He felt better now, though, with the car stopped.

Sherman didn't move. His round shoulders were hunched. "So get out," he said finally. For a moment, Chicky thought about trying to push him out of the car, but he knew how strong Sherman was, and when drunk he was even stronger. Chicky opened the door and got out.

The second it clipped shut, Sherman took off, tires screeching, and careened around the bend of the beach wall. Chicky stood there, shaky, the streetlight above him like a stooped bird, neck curved, stupid. He started down the hill, his sneakers slapping on the soft tar. The car's hum grew fainter as it rounded the cove, its noise carrying across the still, black water. Then, when the sound reached a certain pitch, he heard the crash, and a quick engine rev, then a faraway tinkling of glass.

Chicky bolted. He ran over the dark road, past the streetlights on one side, the beach wall on the other. In his ears was a whirring as he flew along. The car was a dark hump, jacked up on the fire hydrant.

119

Panting, he went to the window. Sherman's head was motionless on the steering wheel.

"Sherman." He reached through the window to touch his brother's shoulder. Slowly, like a ghost, Sherman lifted his head, dazed. There was dark blood striped down his face, and a mess at his mouth. He started groping, like a sleepwalker, for the inside door handle. "Wait," Chicky said. "Are you okay? Are you all right? Wait. Let me go get help."

He started up the hill. "Stay there," he called back. He heard the door open.

"I'm coming," said Sherman.

"No." It was as if Sherman were rising from the dead. "Just wait there."

"Don't tell Dad," Sherman warned. Chicky made out his dark figure stumbling out of the car, then propping himself against it with one arm.

Chicky tore up the hill, up the driveway, around its curves. The porch light was on and the lights in the TV room. When he burst through the front door, everything seemed small. The TV was going quietly.

Delilah and Hal were still up. "There you are," said Delilah. She had her sewing basket out. When she looked a moment longer at him, her expression changed. "What is it?" Hal was bent over the low table, gluing something together, holding Delilah's feet in his lap.

"Sherman crashed the car."

120

"Oh my God." She jumped up. "Are you okay? Where is he?"

"I wasn't in it. I got out before Booth Cove. He hit the hydrant near the Singers'. I told him to stay there, but he—"

They all rushed out, but stopped on the porch. Down on the driveway, coming out of the dark- ness, was Sherman, like a phantom. Delilah took quick steps down the stairs. "My God, Sherman, are you all right?" She put her hand up near his face but wouldn't touch it. "We better get you to a hospital."

Sherman looked distractedly into the darkness. "I gotta go get the car," he said, squinting toward the house. Then he started peering around in the bushes.

"Are you crazy?" said Delilah. "Leave it. Just come inside." She seized his arm, but he shoved her off.

Above them, the window in Caitlin's room opened. "What's going on down there?" she said, her voice creaky with sleep.

No one answered her. Delilah said, "Come on, Sherman, please!"

Caitlin called, more sharply, "What happened?"

Delilah looked up and whispered, "Sherman cracked up the car. I'm trying to get him to come inside."

Caitlin yelled, "Sherman!"

"Ssshhh!" Delilah went. "You'll wake Dad."

Caitlin whispered back, "Well, Dad should be woken."

Delilah turned, frowning, into the shadows. "Sherman, what are you doing?"

He had gotten on Minnie's bike and started to pedal away, weaving across the driveway, his knees jammed against the handlebars. "Gotta go get the car," he said.

"I'm waking Dad," said Caitlin from above. Then the window went rattling down.

"Hal," Delilah pleaded. Hal and Chicky were still on the porch. "Will you come help?"

Hal went down onto the driveway. From the edge of the light came the clatter of the bike falling over. In one motion, Sherman righted it and got back on. Hal strode over and grabbed the handlebars. "Come on, buddy," he said. "We'll get the car later."

Sherman took a look at him and shoved the bike out from under himself. It wheeled away and toppled over. He headed off blindly in the opposite direction. Hal took him by the shoulder and led him up to the porch.

Caitlin came out in her bathrobe. "Dad's coming," she said, moving to let Sherman and Hal pass.

In the hall, Sherman broke away. "Lemme go," he said. He bowled off toward his room. Hal and Delilah rushed after him; he went faster. Right by the steps leading down to the playroom, they caught up

122

with him and tried to drag him back to the kitchen. He tripped and fell.

Caitlin and Chicky, still back in the hall, couldn't see what happened, but they heard Sherman thudding down the steps.

"Oh my God," Delilah said. "He's going to kill himself."

Caitlin touched Chicky gently. "Are you all right?"

He nodded.

Mr. Vincent appeared at the upstairs banister, a blue towel wrapped around his waist.

"Quick, Dad," cried Caitlin. "He needs help."

Mr. Vincent descended the stairs, not saying anything, frowning. They followed him down the hallway. Delilah said, "He won't listen. He's all cut up." Everyone crowded onto the landing. Down on the playroom floor, Sherman was floundering to his knees.

"Can you get up here?" asked Mr. Vincent, staying at the top.

Sherman peered upward with measuring eyes and gripped the banister. "I want to talk to you," he said, enunciating each word carefully.

"Come up here, then," said Mr. Vincent. Sherman hauled himself along the banister, which was an old oar. His father said, "Are you drunk?"

"Yup," said Sherman.

Mr. Vincent turned to Chicky. "Where's the car?"

"Down by the Singers'. He hit a hydrant."

"You okay," Mr. Vincent said, not as a question. His chest was the color of a pale crab shell, yellowish and soft.

Chicky's eyes welled up. "Uh-huh."

Sherman said, "I want ta talk ta you." When Sherman got drunk, he'd get this thug voice.

"Let's take a look at that cut," said Mr. Vincent, heading for the kitchen. "You might need stitches."

Mr. Vincent snapped on the light and went around the table. Delilah tried leading Sherman to the sink, but he brushed her aside, looking only at his father. He leaned heavily against the counter.

Delilah stamped her foot. "Will you *let* me?"

Sherman kept glaring at Mr. Vincent. "You're my faddah," he said, oblivious of everyone else. Caitlin and Chicky hung back by the calendar.

Delilah said, "Dad, will you tell him to let me wash it off?"

Caitlin hugged herself. The bathrobe she had on was an old one of Mum's. "I think we should take him to the hospital," she said.

Sherman's voice was eerie and low. "Are you my faddah or not?"

Mr. Vincent sat down at the head of the table. "Of course I am," he said in his nervous deep voice. He rested his elbows on the table, locked his hands, and rubbed his thumbs together earnestly.

124

They all waited, staying very still. "Then you should act like a faddah," Sherman said.

Everybody looked at him and then at Mr. Vincent. He pushed back his chair and sat up as straight as a rod, the way he did when he was demonstrating posture, and firmly planted his hands on his bare knees. He looked at Sherman and waited.

The thug voice was thick. "Then why don't you never act like it?"

Mr. Vincent stayed stiff. "Like what?"

Sherman stared at him, his head set. Delilah touched his arm and whispered, "Sherman," but he wasn't hearing a thing.

Mr. Vincent stood up. "You're drunk," he said. "I'm not going to talk to someone who's drunk." He tried to go between the table and the counter to leave, but Sherman grabbed his arm, pinching it, making white marks.

"I want ta talk ta you," he said through clenched teeth.

Mr. Vincent yanked his arm away. "Now, cut this out—I'll talk to you when you're sober," he said, disgusted. He hurried out of the room, bumping into stray chairs on the way. All the children turned in the direction of his diminishing footsteps.

Then from Sherman came a kind of wail, a hollow cry like something heard on a marsh, and he looped around at the waist. Delilah tried to calm him, her hands fluttering around as if she were chasing after

125

a bird that had gotten in the house. Caitlin let out a sob and clapped her palm over her mouth, staring at Sherman.

Chicky looked at her. It was like when their mother died. When you first heard the news, when it first hit you, it was like that—you couldn't breathe. It was as if the Devil had appeared for an instant, and you couldn't breathe.

Sherman kept up his wail, his shoulders swaying. As she watched him, Delilah's eyes got wider and wider, and then she began to cry softly. She touched him, saying, "Oh, Shermy. Oh, honey." Then she got taken over by her own crying and turned to Hal and put her face into his chest and her shoulders shook up and down and her neck showed where the hair parted.

Chicky stepped past them and went to the back door and opened it and stood there. The crickets outside, a million of them, were ticking *reek reek reek* in the dark. He turned back around.

Then it wasn't the same anymore as when their mother had died. It wasn't as if you had seen the Devil only in a flash. It wasn't as if he had appeared for an instant and then was gone again. Now the feeling was this: that the Devil had swooped down and had landed and was lingering with them all, hulking in the middle of the kitchen table, settling down to stay.

126

WEDLOCK

The church was looking cheerful for once. All the altar candles were lit and wound with red ribbon. There were white poinsettias in silver pots. It was Christmas, the first Christmas since Mum died. The Vincents came in late. The girls bustled down the aisle with pale and harried faces. The boys followed, slow-booted and hulking, hitting the bench backs with large hands. Gus had a cast on his nose, Sherman wasn't wearing a coat, and Chicky looked haunted and emaciated, a fourteen-year-old after his first term at boarding school. Gus had broken his nose in a hockey game.

Behind his seven children came Dad in his parka.

He wasn't used to being in church, not being Catholic; the rest of them led the way.

Their pews—the ones Mum always chose—were free. Caitlin genuflected, and sidled in. Delilah touched her forehead with deeper feeling. Minnie, waist-high to her sisters, shuffled into the pew, guided by Sophie. She had let Minnie do her own pigtails that morning and the result was a wayward, tentative part up the back of her seven-year-old head. Sophie crossed herself carelessly, having lost interest in many things. Up at the altar, the priest, hands spread, was warming himself at an invisible fire.

No one looked directly at Dad, but each knew where he was. He joined the boys in the second pew.

Near the end of Mass, the priest said, "Let us now offer each other the sign of peace." A woman behind them in a quilted coat whispered, "I'm glad to see you all together." Dad looked disturbed and thanked her awkwardly.

It was still raining when they drove home. The house seemed to float on the top of the hill like an island at the edge of the sea. It wasn't cold enough for snow, though the dampness made it seem so and everything had a chill. They lit a fire in the living room and went through the presents fast.

The girls had bought all the presents, including the presents for themselves. Minnie got lots of presents, the boys got lots of socks. Just what I wanted! and

128

How did you know! Everyone was miserable. Gus festooned his head with ribbons. Dad decided it was too dangerous to burn the wrapping paper as they had always done, and was rolling it into balls and stuffing them into a huge trash can he'd carried up from the basement.

They ate ravenously at lunch. Silence hung between the tinkling of silverware, and with the rain streaming down the long French windows it was like being underwater. The flames of the candles were transparent in the odd gray light. Caitlin brought up Pat Meyer in a polite tone. Dad pushed his plate away and looked terrified. "You should ask her over later," Caitlin said. Dad wiped his mouth with a napkin, regarding each of his children suspiciously.

After lunch, everyone fell asleep. For hours the house was quiet except for the sound of breathing. The rain kept up. It rained in long lashes, coming down and drumming on the lawn, moving over the roof then out to sea, where it appeared in windy bruises over the surface. The islands out there had names like Desolation or Cold Point. Another island was Stillman's.

When they awoke the fires had all gone out and they'd lost all sense of time. It was beginning to get dark. The trees seemed to move together and huddle in nets of mist. Everyone ended up in the kitchen, switching on the lights and starting water for tea.

They took out the cookie tins and baking dishes that had arrived all week, left on the hall table or the kitchen counter by people from town. *Love to all the Vincents* the cards said inside berry borders, from the Paul Habits, the Harry Finches, Isabel Millicent and her dog Carlyle, the house-sitters Alex and Ann. They got a fruitcake from Mrs. Salieri, who hadn't cleaned for them in years, and chocolate sailboats from the hairdressers at Phil's.

Gus took out the turkey, what was left of it.

Sophie stared at the pans lying upside down on the counter. "Doesn't it seem kind of pathetic—just us?"

"What do you mean?" said Caitlin. "We're a family."

"Yah, but it doesn't feel like we're all here."

"We're not," Chicky said.

"Joanie Nathan said the first year needs to go by before you get used to it," Caitlin said.

"We have a month, then," Chicky said. It had been eleven months since the accident.

"I'm not expecting to *get* used to it," said Delilah with disgust.

"Well, it feels like more than just Mum," Sophie said.

Everyone nodded. It wasn't just one thing, a thousand things were missing. The house was filled with missing things, despite the Christmas decorations being up. The girls hadn't known where the decorations were, but Minnie showed them. There were other discoveries in the back room, things they hadn't seen in a long time. The pink evening dress with the jeweled top, chiffon skirts, flowered muumuus from Mum's pregnancy days. There was a shoebox of postcards from Mr. Kittredge. The girls put the decorations where they always got put—the crèche on the Chinese table in the hall, the laurel looping down the banister, the wooden fruit poked into wreaths. They taped Christmas cards to the stair railing the way Mum had and lit the pine candle. Nothing was the same.

Dad walked in, puffy-eyed, with his jacket on.

"How're you?" Caitlin asked with an odd look.

"Couldn't be better," he said. He looked awful. He walked out the door.

"What's his problem?" Caitlin said.

"Leave him alone," Sophie said. "The guy's wife is dead, okay?"

Delilah frowned. "Some people's mothers are dead too."

They heard the car start.

"You can get another wife," Gus said, selecting pieces of turkey for his sandwich. "You can't get another mother."

Caitlin watched him; his cast made him look cross-eyed.

131

"I just asked what's his problem."

"Where'd he go anyway?" Sophie said.

"Maybe to see Pat," Caitlin said.

"Let's hope," Sophie said.

"For our sake," Caitlin said. She and Sophie laughed.

"He went to get shaving cream," Delilah said and gave Sophie a particular look. "He said he used to get it in his stocking."

"I forgot," Sophie said. "I forgot the shaving cream."

"If we'd done the stockings together . . ." said Delilah, sighing deeply.

Caitlin sipped her tea from her spoon. "Well, I wish he'd just marry her."

"You think?" Gus said. He sampled a scrap of meat.

"Will you please close your mouth while you're eating?" said Delilah, unable to look.

"I could see it," Sophie said. "I think it would be good."

Delilah shook her head. This wasn't even worth talking about. "No way," she said.

"I don't see why he doesn't bring her over," Caitlin said.

"I do," said Gus. His sandwich was now higher than it was wide.

"I wouldn't if I were him," Sherman said.

The girls seemed to consider this for a moment. "Well, I don't think it's normal," Caitlin said finally.

"You guys are always cutting up Dad," said Minnie in her soft voice. Everyone's eyebrows rose in surprise. Minnie was staring into her mug, an inch away from it.

Delilah's arm stretched across the table, just short of Minnie. "No we're not, honey. We're just talking about him."

Minnie tried to tighten her mouth and her chin trembled. "Well maybe you should talk about yourselves," she said.

"Atta girl, Min," said Gus proudly. Hearing this, Minnie colored deeply and seemed about to cry.

"How do you expect to eat that thing, Gus?" Delilah said.

"Easily." He took a bite.

"Would you at least mind closing your mouth?"

Sherman's attention had for some time been directed into the pantry. "Something's the matter with the cats," he said.

Caitlin tossed her hand up. "So what else is new?"

"They're always weird," Delilah said. She turned around and spotted one coming straight for her. "Get away from me!" she screamed. She sat up stiffly and shivered. "I'm sorry," she said. "They give me the creeps."

"Have you fed them?" Caitlin asked Sherman.

"Have *you?*" Chicky put in. Everyone looked at him.

Caitlin shook her head wearily. She'd never have peace.

Sherman continued to watch the cats. They were all black, the only kind Mum would have. They moved about the house soundlessly. They jumped off tables and chairs without a noise, as if they were moving in a tank, their paws hardly touching down. Sometimes they came at you, their eyes with a certain look. They wanted something from you and knew how to get it. Sherman said, "It's like they're Mum."

Delilah turned to him with annoyance. Then she seemed to understand what he meant. Chicky was nodding; he'd heard this before. Outside the rain picked up and the gutters rattled and there was splashing from the waterspout arching past the window by the sink.

Caitlin inspected the stamp on a bit of shortbread. "Maybe he did go see Pat," she said.

Much later the girls found themselves alone in the living room. Minnie was tucked into bed, guarded by her new hockey skates. The lights of the Christmas tree were reflected in the long black windows.

"Thank the Lord that day is over with," said Sophie. "Though he's probably not the one I should thank."

"It wasn't that bad," said Caitlin, peeling tags off things in her lap.

"It wasn't?" said Sophie, motionless in an armchair.

"Jesus, Sophie. You're always bringing up the worst side." Delilah was lying on her stomach on the sofa, her cheek mashed against a pillow. "Sophie?" She was unable to see her. She heaved herself up, twisted around, and met Sophie's eye. "Well you do," she said and flopped back down.

Sophie changed the subject. "How was Eliot?" she asked Caitlin.

"Fine," said Caitlin. Then more warmly: "Fine."

Sophie and Delilah waited.

"We had another fight, though."

"What about?"

"Oh, the usual."

Delilah nodded.

"I don't know." Caitlin sighed. "Who knows what's going to happen."

"What is?" Sophie asked.

"What do you want—me to get married tomorrow?"

"You're the one wants to get married, Caitlin."

"Eventually maybe." This was too exasperating. "Frankly, I'm not sure he's the one."

"I'm sure Hal's the one," Delilah said, hugging a pillow. "My sugie."

"Here's a new tune," Sophie said. Delilah had hung up on Hal the night before during their nightly call. When he called back, no one was allowed to answer it. It rang and rang. Finally Dad picked up the receiver upstairs and without saying hello, set it down.

"I talked to him today," Delilah said with a private smile.

"Luckily I don't have to worry about it," Sophie said.

"Come off it," Caitlin said—an age-old subject. "There just aren't a whole lot of men in Marshport." All three laughed. "Anyway it's your own doing, living at home."

"Somebody has to."

"Says who? We could have gotten a housekeeper like the Nathans, only nobody else wanted to."

"Could *you* see Dad?" Delilah said.

"And what about Minnie?" Sophie said.

"Have it your way," Caitlin said. "I don't care."

Sophie stood up and went to the window and looked out at the forgotten world. "It's stopped raining," she said. It was freezing out there, everything icing over. Tomorrow the lawn would be as hard as rock.

Caitlin leaned her head back and looked upside

down at the window. "Remember how she used to make us stand there and watch the lightning?"

"She acted like it was this fun thing," said Sophie.

"And she was scared of it," said Caitlin.

"Like with the MG," Delilah said. " 'Here we go, monkeys!' she screams, like we're on a joyride, then smashes us into the wall."

Caitlin's head was still back, her throat stretched long. "I felt grown-up carrying the groceries home. . . . What a funny thing to do with the thunder. . . ."

A noise came from the doorway. A white triangle appeared in the gloom of the hall. " 'Night," said the low voice. " 'Night, Goatie," said the girls, using Mum's nickname. Gus retreated down the hall to the maid's room where the boys had their midnight smoke. His footsteps went without hesitation even in the dark.

Thuds were heard above them.

"Uh-oh," said Sophie.

Someone was coming down the stairs. The girls waited. Dad appeared in the doorway. He never wore pajamas and they were used to that. Still, they looked away. Without his glasses, he couldn't see a thing. He frowned—a perplexed caveman at the mouth of his cave.

Caitlin cleared her throat. Sophie adjusted a pillow, set down an ashtray. Dad wasn't hearing any of it. His ear was cocked though, listening for something else.

"They're going to get me," he said. But no, that was wrong. He shook his head.

Caitlin, pushing at her cuticles, said, "Go back to bed, Dad."

He turned back obediently. Before going back up the stairs, something occurred to him. "Extraordinary children," he said, holding very still, then was gone.

The girls studied one another. Sophie whispered, "He had a lot tonight." Then Delilah whispered in a different tone, "Kooks!" and made her Aunt Mo face and everyone began to smile. But their smiles wouldn't quite take and their faces wouldn't quite go.

They lapsed into vacant stares, fixing on objects in the room. Sophie gazed at the tree. The ornaments had been collected over the years. Decorating the tree, they had lifted them out of the boxes—the silk pear, the glass bulb with the angel inside, gilded pinecones, the red and green and silver balls that stretched your reflection, holding them by the hooks. Mum had had a certain way of cocking her wrist, with a finger out, dangling the ornament while she decided where it should go. This year, decorating the tree themselves, it was as if they had Mum's hands. The tree was approached by hundreds of Mum's hands.

Delilah was eyeing a cigarette box. Sophie noticed

and picked it up off the table. "I used to think this was the most amazing thing—writing in silver." The signatures of the ushers in their parents' wedding were engraved on the lid.

There was a crash above them in Dad's room.

"It's easy to get done," Caitlin said. "You just get the people to sign their names, then give it to the jeweler."

"I can't believe you forgot the shaving cream, Soph," said Delilah.

Sophie winced and continued looking at the silver box.

Caitlin went on, "We did it for Torey Adams when she got married—all the bridesmaids. We'll do it for you, Soph." Caitlin added brightly, "On your wedding day."

Sophie dropped the silver box as if it were electrified. They all laughed. "Right," said Sophie and their laughter increased. "Right." They shook their heads as the hilarity dawned on them. "Me too!" said Delilah. They were gasping for breath. "Me too!" They had to close their eyes. Their hands, helpless, waved languidly in the air. Imagine—getting married. They couldn't stop laughing and laughed till they were exhausted. None of them would be getting married for a long time.

▼

There was nothing left to do but go to bed. They sighed, piling up their boxes, setting perfume bottles on their sides. Delilah tucked matches into her cigarettes, picked up her boots.

"You need taps on those," Caitlin said. "They're wrecked now. But next time."

"They're not wrecked. They just look wrecked."

"It's okay," said Caitlin. "But in the future . . ."

Sophie pulled out the lights on the tree.

"Awww, leave it on," Delilah said.

"All night?"

"Mum used to."

"Not after Christmas though," Caitlin said.

They left the tree dark. Huddling in the doorway at the bottom of the stairs, they looked back into the room to make sure they hadn't forgotten anything. There were only dark shapes now. Through the far windows they could see the lights of Andre's Point across the water. "Come on," Caitlin said. She sounded muffled and distant. It was as if the rain that had streamed down the windows all the day was now filling the house, swirling in around them. They held their breaths. Sophie nudged Delilah and Delilah turned and blinked. Everything looked blurry. They all began to move but it was not so easy and still they did not move right away.

140

THOROFARE

"I'm not about to trust this guy," said Delilah after the undertaker excused himself from the reception room. She craned her neck and peered down the hall after him. They could hear cabinets whining open and snapping shut.

"He can't find her," she said. Delilah did not like being waited on.

"Be quiet," said Sophie. "He'll hear you."

"I don't care," she whispered, frustrated. "What's taking him so long?"

"Maybe after a while they lose track. Most people probably aren't left here so long."

"That's for sure," Delilah said, and rolled her eyes.

For a year and a half after Mum died, Dad had avoided the subject of her ashes, and they remained at the funeral home. Now, a month after remarrying, he'd asked Sophie and Delilah, who was home after graduating from college, to pick them up.

Delilah resumed her watch, her mouth slack with fascination. Sophie turned away from her and went to the bay window. It was May, and across the street kids in a playground were having a muddy recess, pushing each other over and screaming. Inside where the sisters were, it was quiet. A few chairs were lined up against the wall. Sophie's heart was doing peculiar, anxious things.

"Finally," whispered Delilah. Sophie turned back to see her swinging her boot nonchalantly.

The undertaker came out with a white box. "Here you are, Miss Vincent," he said. He seemed young for an undertaker. His beige hair was sprayed into place.

Delilah eyed him. "Are you sure it's her?"

He smiled without showing his teeth and didn't answer.

Sophie took the box. It was cardboard, a little taller than an ice-cream carton, and narrower.

"How do you know?" Delilah asked.

"There is a card," he sighed.

The girls exchanged glances and stood there dumbly, unsure of how to proceed.

142

"Is that it?" Sophie said.

"Yes," he said. "Everything else has been taken care of."

By whom they couldn't imagine. It wasn't exactly Dad's thing.

Outside was a weak sun. They got into the car that Sophie drove—the one Dad had bought when she moved home to take care of Minnie. Sophie handed the box to Delilah in the passenger seat. "It's heavy," she said, wanting to say something normal.

Delilah's face was pale. She placed the box in her lap. "I can't believe this is her," she said.

"It's not."

"I know." She stared off. "But you know what I mean."

They drove through the small streets of Marshport. It was the middle of the day, and there was little traffic—repair trucks, and station wagons with housewives in them. The car wound along the shore, going in and out of sight of the ocean—Boston's tiny skyline far away to the south—passing the stone walls, the hidden mansions.

"Should we look inside?" Sophie asked. Sophie observed her hands on the steering wheel; they seemed separate, someone else's hands.

Delilah lit a cigarette and threaded the match through a crack in the window. She took a deep

143

drag. Sophie held out two fingers and Delilah handed it over. "Okay," she said.

She untucked the top; it was flimsy, with a zigzag edge. She picked out a card and held it up by the dashboard so Sophie could see. It said *Rose Marie Vincent* in script.

"Jesus," Sophie said.

"Slow down, Sophie," Delilah said. "You're as bad as Gus." Gus had cracked up the same car twice.

"What's in it?" Sophie asked, keeping her eyes on the road.

"A Baggie." She slid it out by its knot. "Weird," she said. "It's all white chunks."

Sophie shuddered. "It's the bones."

Delilah peered closer, undaunted. "You know, they kind of look like shells."

"Oh God, Delou," Sophie said and held out the cigarette. Without looking over Delilah took it back.

The morning Mum died, they were gathered in the dim light of the TV room. Dad was a wreck, mute, his face bloated. The boys were on the couch, Gus in the middle, with a hand on each brother's knee. Sherman and Chicky were staring dumbly ahead. Sophie stood in front of the dark fireplace. She'd just returned from visiting college friends to find the driveway crowded with cars. Two hours before, on her way to the market, Mum's car had been hit by a train. The shock had been absolute. Sophie held on to the low mantelpiece, steadying herself. Now they were discussing the funeral. She told Dad, "She wanted to be cremated." It came out level, flat.

No further devastation could have shown on his face. "She did?"

Everything was different—another world suddenly. The boys looked as if all the air had been socked out of them. Minnie had been taken out of first grade and was staying with some friends for the day.

"Yes, she wanted her ashes sprinkled in the thorofare. I remember her saying so last summer."

Dad looked at Sophie with horror. People were passing by the doorway, mixing in the hall, whispering and then drifting away when they saw the dark conference. Sophie felt weightless and hollow, moving through it all like some strange pillar. Back in the kitchen, Mum's friends were making ham sandwiches on the Vincents' carving board. The men were wearing their business suits. Caitlin was on her way home from New York, where she'd moved after college. Delilah, in Florida with her boyfriend Hal, didn't even know yet.

Ellen Grady, one of their only Catholic friends, was in the TV room with them. "I'm not sure cremation's allowed in the Church," she said timidly. So-

145

phie looked at her. Mum was dead. Sophie turned to Dad. "I know it's what she wanted." The kids, like Mum, were Catholic. Dad didn't know about any of this; he didn't know where to look.

While she could be cremated, the body had to be present at the funeral Mass. The casket was hidden with a covering of daffodils. They wanted a dress to put her in. Caitlin, Delilah, and Sophie went through Mum's closets. Caitlin pulled one from the hanger.

"But I love that dress," Delilah said. It was lilac blue with little block prints. "And they're just going to burn it."

"It was her favorite though," Caitlin said.

They all stared at it, and slowly began to nod.

Delilah put the ashes away in the sideboard in the dining room. The whirring in the kitchen was Pat, Dad's new wife, making dinner. When they were little, Pat had been a friend of Mum's, one of the mothers always smiling. When Pat got divorced and went to work in Boston, Mum tried to fix her up with someone a couple of times, but it didn't work out. The summer after Mum died, Pat started asking Dad out to lunch in Faneuil Market.

When Dad got home from work, he went straight to the hall table. "We got Mum's ashes," Sophie told him while he was leafing through the mail.

He showed her a blank face. "Thank you," he said.

Delilah came around the corner. "Don't you want to see them?" she asked.

He cleared his throat. "Certainly," he said.

She led him off toward the dining room. "See?" Sophie heard her say. "They kind of look like shells."

Sophie went into the living room, where no one ever went. Pat had taken down the curtains to be cleaned, and the yellow sunset came flooding through the French doors. A silver cigarette box on the glass table caught the light and sent it shooting into a high corner. There was a new painting—one Pat had brought—hanging over the couch. The rug was gone, revealing a polished wooden floor Sophie had never seen before. During the past year, when the house had been under her care, things had deteriorated. Already, Pat had brought painters in for the upstairs bedrooms, and Mr. Parsons had been over to look at the rot on the front porch.

Sophie sat on the arm of a chair. She couldn't make out everything that Dad and Delilah were saying, but could hear her sister's voice working itself into a high pitch. Then she heard Dad's "No."

Immediately, Delilah was tearing up the stairs. "But she's my mother too!" she cried.

Out in the hall Sophie ran into Minnie, wide-eyed, with Sherman and Chicky hovering behind her.

"What's her problem?" said Chicky. At fifteen, he

was the youngest of the boys, gangly and awkward, with dark, nervous eyes. His hand plucked at tufts of hair.

Upstairs a door slammed. Sherman stood there, hulking, silent as usual. Sophie glimpsed Dad at the end of the corridor, aiming for the kitchen.

"Delilah thinks we should scatter some of Mum's ashes here," Sophie said. "Dad's not wild about the idea."

"Why not?" said Minnie.

"You never know, hon."

"I thought we were bringing them to Maine," said Sherman, deadpan.

"We are." Sophie touched his shoulder. It was rock-hard; he flinched.

They were leaving the next morning. Every Memorial Day weekend, the Vincents opened the house in North Eden. This trip, they were taking Mum's ashes to throw in the thorofare, the channel that ran between the islands.

Caitlin appeared on the stairs. "Are we fighting already?" She had come up that afternoon from New York, where she'd just started working in an ad agency. She was changed into her regular clothes.

"It's Dad and Delilah," Sophie said.

"Oh," Caitlin said, as if that explained it.

They went into the TV room to watch the news. Everyone except Gus was home that night. He was up in Maine already, in college, and would meet them the next day at the North Eden ferry. Sophie and Chicky were on the couch, their feet up on the table next to the neat stacks of magazines. Minnie lay on the floor, coloring, while Caitlin tried to make conversation with Sherman. How was school? Fine. How was lacrosse? All right. Sophie told her Sherman was high scorer. "That's great," Caitlin said, hitting a pillow. "Good for you." Sherman kept his eyes on the TV. Chicky was flipping through *Life*. When he turned the pages, Sophie noticed his fingers trembling.

About twenty minutes later Dad stood in the hall and bellowed up the stairs for Delilah. Everyone in the TV room kept quiet and listened.

"What?" came her suffering voice. She was probably collapsed on her bed.

"Come down here," said Dad.

"Why?"

"Come down here," he repeated.

Footsteps crossed the ceiling above them, then were heard thumping down the stairs. "What do you want?" she said.

"Come with me," he said matter-of-factly.

The footsteps stopped. "*Where,* Dad?"

He was perfectly calm. "Come along."

She let out a huge sigh and continued heavily down the steps. "I'm coming, but where?"

149

The screen door opened and they went outside on the terrace.

Caitlin leaned down to Minnie. "See where they're going." Minnie hopped up, and her pigtailed head disappeared around the door.

They waited for her to return. "They're by Dad's garden," she said eagerly.

Caitlin took her by the elbows and studied her face. "What are they doing?"

"Okay," she said, and went out again. This time she spoke from the hall. "They've got the box with Mum's ashes." They all got up and went into the hall.

There was a narrow window on either side of the door. They clustered at one, to stay out of sight. Dad and Delilah were standing at the edge of the lawn. Behind them the spring trees made a light-green screen, and beyond it the ocean was flat. Dad held the box while Delilah reached inside. She pulled back her fist and flung some white bits over the garden and down the hill. Dad's chin was drawn in against his Adam's apple, his mouth peculiar and tight. When Delilah turned back toward the house, her eyes were dark and glassy. Everyone ducked away before she noticed them watching.

Pat made a huge meal that night for dinner—rack of lamb and biscuits and a lemon soufflé pie. Somehow she kept her neat size-six figure. Dad, however, had already put on a few pounds.

150

▼

They drove up in two cars. Caitlin and Minnie went with Dad and Pat in the station wagon. Delilah and Sophie took the boys, who slept in the back the whole way. They had the box with Mum's ashes in their car.

Gus and his girlfriend, Sarah, were already at the ferry landing, sitting on their knapsacks. He gave Sophie a bear hug. He pulled the hat off Chicky's head and put it on his own.

"How'd you get here?" said Caitlin.

"Hitched," said Gus cheerfully.

"What?" said Sherman, regarding him levelly. "You trying to grow a beard?"

Gus shrugged.

"Dad'll love that," said Delilah.

Gus put his arm around Sarah. "Well good for Dad," he said.

Buying the tickets, Caitlin said, "I should have brought Eliot."

"I thought you broke up," Sophie said.

"We did," she said. "Kind of. I don't know what's going on."

The ferry was still running on the winter schedule. Despite the cold, they stood at the upper railing the whole ride over, their hair and collars flapping, and pointed out the islands to Sarah—Barnacle Island,

151

Seabrook Hills, the Dumplings—and passed the gong. The bay was choppy and gray and flashing with sun. Pat stayed in the car and read magazines while Dad, who could never sit still, walked back and forth between his children and her.

The lilacs had just come out in Maine, and forget-me-nots were tangled in the grass behind the laundry room. The house was once a warehouse, set at the edge of a wide dock, with bay windows only inches above the water at high tide. There were signs of winter wear—the piling supports under the living room were awry—and flooding had left a watermark on the wainscoting in the downstairs hall.

The next day, it was bright out and blustery. In the morning, Caitlin and Sophie took their mugs of tea out and sat on the dock under the empty window boxes, out of the wind.

Delilah came out, trying not to spill her coffee. "She's in there making lobster gumbo already," she said.

"Where are the boys?" asked Caitlin. She tilted her face to the white sky and closed her eyes.

"Still sacked out." Delilah put a cigarette between her lips and tried to light matches against the wind.

Through the railing they could see Dad down on the float getting the boat ready. "He wants to go as soon as they're up," Sophie said.

"Which will be forever," said Caitlin, her eyes still shut.

Sophie took Delilah's cigarette and lit it for her by turning away, crouching near the shingles. She handed it back. "Is Pat coming with us?" she asked.

Delilah dragged on her cigarette and looked at Sophie, alarmed. "No. Why should she?"

"I don't know. I just thought maybe . . ."

Caitlin said, "Yah. I was wondering, too."

"No way," Delilah said. "Just the family. Sarah's not coming either."

Sophie regarded Caitlin. "Do you think you're getting any sun?"

"Yes," she said defensively.

"No way," said Gus, coming around the corner. He arched his back and yawned, stretching. "No . . . waay. . . ."

Caitlin opened her eyes. "It's about time you got up," she said.

Usually, loading everybody into the boat was a major operation. They scrambled and fought for seats, balancing books and towels and the iced-tea cooler, arguing about where to take the picnic, ordering the boys to cast off, making Minnie do up her life jacket. Today they moved through it as if the ground were eggshells.

Dad waited at the controls. Minnie crawled into

153

Gus's lap and nestled in his bulky jacket. Delilah, with the white box, stood at Dad's side. Chicky was on the dock, his hair blowing in his eyes, keeping an unsteady hold on the bow railing while Sherman untied the stern. It was all done without a sound. Sherman tossed the rope in over the gas tanks and stepped in stiffly, looking down.

"Sherman, aren't you going to be cold?" Caitlin said. They were bundled in sweaters and hats; Sherman wasn't wearing anything over his flannel shirt. He didn't answer and sat down heavily on the seat in front of the Plexiglas windshield.

"Sherman," she said in a gentle voice. "It's going to be cold out there."

He folded his thick arms across his chest and gave her a neutral look. "Okay, Caitlin," he said.

Even though there were few boats in the harbor, Dad waited till they were well out of the moorings before pushing the boat into full throttle. The gray water sped by, the surface waves crisscrossing. Going by the first point, they passed the Washburns' house, with its windows boarded up. When they entered the wider thorofare, the stronger wind hit with a blast. To the north was the rolling shore of North Eden, and south were the uninhabited islands, lined up toward the east: Driftwood, Black Island, Fling, Storm Head.

The boat began to slow down. Sherman made a

154

face against the wind; Caitlin started scratching at something on her dungarees. The bow fell slightly, and Delilah gazed back over the stern, where the wake was flattening out. Dad, holding his chin high, continued to look forward, checking for lobster pots. Gus's hands were cupped over his mouth, warming them, his eyes cast to the side. Chicky glanced back and forth between Dad and where they were heading, to see which spot he'd choose. Tentatively, Minnie hoisted herself from Gus's lap and tried to look interested in something over the side of the boat.

They puttered along this way slowly for a while.

"This is good," Delilah said, but Dad went on surveying the surrounding water. Sophie turned Minnie around and held her shoulders from behind.

The waves smacked the sides when the engine went into idle. After Dad cut the motor, the boat spun slightly and dipped in and out of the swells, and it was suddenly quiet except for the wind. Chicky gave Gus a hand-up off the floor. All faces turned to Dad.

Delilah was opening the flap of the box; Dad took it from her, extracting the bag himself.

"All right," he said. "Minnie first." He held the bag from underneath.

Sophie eased Minnie toward him; Minnie hesitated. "What'll I do?" she said.

155

Dad lowered the bag near the side.

Sophie said, "Just take a handful, Min."

Caitlin smoothed one of her pigtails. "Just take a little, honey, and throw it over."

"How?" Minnie held her palm up flat. Her clear eyes were watering over.

"It's okay," said Gus. "Just take as much as you can."

Minnie looked at Dad and kept blinking. He held out the bag.

Chicky moved her aside. "Here," he said. "I'll go and show her." His lanky hand went into the bag and grappled awkwardly. It looked for a moment as if he and Dad were struggling with each other. Pressing his free hand against the side of the bag, Chicky pulled out a handful of ashes. When he threw them, low, the heavier bits landed scuttling in a line, and the wind carried the finer white dust a little way through the air. He bent down to Minnie. "There," he said in his trembling voice. "See?"

Dad lowered the bag and she put in her tiny hand, drew out a tight fist, and threw an exuberant overhand, releasing it late, so it shot into the water just inches from the boat. She gave everyone a pleading embarrassed look.

"That was fine," Sophie said, and touched her sleeve. "You want to do it again?" She shook her head, chewing on her bottom lip.

"Sherman," Dad said. They were going by age now.

Sherman always had the strongest throw. When they skipped rocks off the beach, his stone would go skittering farther than anyone else's. He took his handful, keeping a distance from the bag, as if it were contaminated. He tossed the ashes loosely and didn't bother to see where they landed.

Gus frowned in his direction and moved up. He fitted both hands into the bag, pulled them out, and then let them go like a golf swing, flinging the ashes in a great arc. With the wind, they speckled down like rain.

"Wow," said Delilah facetiously.

She went next, keeping her back straight. Her features were solemn and composed. She took two careful handfuls, one after the other, and, lifting one foot off the floor as if she were spreading grass seed over a lawn, sprinkled them over the surface of the water. She stepped out of the way.

Sophie slid both hands into the bag and brought them out cupped together in a bowl. Before letting go, she looked at the knobby pieces and saw they weren't flat like shells, but rounded and porous, like little ruins. She leaned way out and let them pour off the ends of her fingers, watching them sink in the dark water, thinking, This is just like anything else you throw overboard—the way it falls in slow mo-

157

tion and then suddenly it's gone, so gradually you can't tell the exact moment it disappears from sight.

Caitlin followed. She was graceful, efficient, staring at the water afterward, her eyebrows peaked, her lips pressed tightly together.

Dad took a handful, quickly, gave it a toss, then held the bag upside down over the water and shook it out. A fine white dust swirled through the air, and he shook the bag and shook it again, till the plastic was clean. Then he swiftly balled it up with two fast hands and shoved it into his pocket.

They kissed each other then, or some of them did. Sophie kissed Minnie under her eye, and took Gus's hand to squeeze. Caitlin and she exchanged looks— there was some awkward bumbling—Sherman apart, up near the bow, and Chicky nervously trying to smile. Delilah moved up to Dad, and he took her kiss on his cheek, bending his knees while he started up the engine. The sky was breaking up, and white swirls shone through like marble.

They sped back to the inner thorofare. Caitlin turned around to Dad, her hair wrapping across her face, and shouted, "Do you think it will get nice?" She pointed ahead.

"I know it will," said Dad, steering straight, his eyes slitted against the wind.

When they got back to the dock, the light had become less opaque and the air was warmer. Sunlight was showing up with the sharpening shadows. They unloaded onto the dock, wind-tousleed and strangely exhilarated. Dad went into reverse—having dropped them off—and putted out by himself to leave the boat at the mooring. Up the ramp they went, in single file, feeling something lofty in their procession, hearing flags billow and snap, following at one another's heels, no one with the slightest idea, when they raised their heads and looked around, of where to go next.